Stories by Contemporary Writers from Shanghai

THERE IS
NO IF

T0095715

This book is edited and designed by the Editorial Committee of *Cultural China* series

Text by Su De
Translation by Zhu Jingwen
Cover Image by Quanjing
Interior Design by Xue Wenqing
Cover Design by Wang Wei

Assistant Editor: Hou Weiting
Editors: Wu Yuezhou, Susan Luu Xiang
Editorial Director: Zhang Yicong

Senior Consultants: Sun Yong, Wu Ying, Yang Xinci
Managing Director and Publisher: Wang Youbu

ISBN: 978-1-60220-243-6

Address any comments about *There Is No If* to:

Better Link Press
99 Park Ave
New York, NY 10016
USA

or

Shanghai Press and Publishing Development Company
F 7 Donghu Road, Shanghai, China (200031)
Email: comments_betterlinkpress@hotmail.com

Printed in China by Shanghai Donnelley Printing Co., Ltd.

1   3   5   7   9   10   8   6   4   2

THERE IS
NO IF

By Su De

Better Link Press

Foreword

This collection of books for English readers consists of short stories and novellas published by writers based in Shanghai. Apart from a few who are immigrants to Shanghai, most of them were born in the city, from the latter part of the 1940s to the 1980s. Some of them had their works published in the late 1970s and the early 1980s; some gained recognition only in the 21st century. The older among them were the focus of the "To the Mountains and Villages" campaign in their youth, and as a result, lived and worked in the villages. The difficult paths of their lives had given them unique experiences and perspectives prior to their eventual return to Shanghai. They took up creative writing for different reasons but all share a creative urge and a love for writing. By profession, some of them are college professors, some literary editors, some directors of literary institutions, some freelance writers and some professional writers. From the individual styles of the authors and the art of their writings, readers can easily detect traces of the authors' own experiences in life, their interests, as well as their aesthetic values. Most of the works in this collection are still written in the realistic style that represents, in a painstakingly fashioned fictional world, the changes of the times in urban and rural life. Having grown up in a more open era, the younger writers have been spared the hardships experienced by their predecessors, and therefore seek greater freedom in their writing. Whatever category of writers they belong to, all of them have gained their rightful places in the Chinese literary circles over the last forty years. Shanghai writers tend to favor urban narratives more than other genres of writing. Most of the works in this collection can be characterized as urban literature with Shanghai characteristics, but there are also exceptions.

Called the "Paris of the East," Shanghai was already an international metropolis in the 1920s and 30s. Being the center of China's economy, culture and literature at the time, it housed a majority of writers of importance in the history of modern Chinese literature. The list includes Lu Xun, Guo Moruo, Mao Dun and Ba Jin, who had all written and published prolifically in Shanghai. Now, with Shanghai re-emerging as a globalized metropolis, the Shanghai writers who have appeared on the literary scene in the last forty years all face new challenges and literary quests of the times. I am confident that some of the older writers will produce new masterpieces. As for the fledging new generation of writers, we naturally expect them to go far in their long writing careers ahead of them. In due course, we will also introduce those writers who did not make it into this collection.

Wang Jiren
Series Editor

Contents

There Is No If

1

Daylight just arrived outside. Xiqing turned and saw the morning sunshine streaming in from the narrow openings of the drapery. Her eyes felt dry. She blinked hard a few times, the nerves deep inside once again got tangled together. The odor of alcohol could still be smelled in the air. Lu Weijun's puppy Luka with its rear end holding high came in through the drapery and let in a wide swatch of sunshine. The light came in so fast as if something glittering just fell swishing to the ground. Lu Weijun was roused by the sound. He sleepily turned his head and was hit by the seven o'clock sun right on. He then realized that nothing fell to the ground but sunshine. Xiqing could see a sparrow on top of Luka's behind on the other side of the window, a fat sparrow who was leaping and pecking diligently, seemingly very happy. Sparrows were the most cherished sight for Xiqing, but to dispel the sense of bleakness they had to appear in groups of three or five. Therefore, however happy this one lonely bird might look, she could still feel the inescapable approach of winter. Lu Weijun extended a hand from behind her and forcefully pulled her in tightly against him. What were you thinking? Lost in your thoughts again? Lu Weijun asked her. He then moved his body once again and came on top of her with all his weight.

Xiqing noticed the tiny dusts around her were flying in all directions circling the straight lines of the sun's rays. She could smell the alcohol in Lu Weijun's mouth, the Piemonte red wine that she brought last night. There was still less than half a bottle left by the TV stand, and if you look closely you could also find some stains on the carpet. She responded half-heartedly, I was thinking it would really be nice to have some red wine in winter. Lu Weijun permed his hair recently, the puffy hair and facial stubble seemed to suit him well. There are people who look themselves only with the right outfit, or they will look like someone else and not themselves. Xiqing touched the lower lip of Lu Weijun with her hand. The parched lip now had turned dark red by the red wine. It really looks good, she thought.

Were you thinking of the wonderful time we may have after drinking the red wine? Lu Weijun lowered his eyes, his lips slipped through her fingers and with his head down he started kissing her in earnest, his body was still hot to the touch. But his response somehow got on Xiqing's nerves. She nimbly patted on his head with her hand and said, I need to take a shower. Then, as if she was flipping a corpse, she unloaded the man who was over her and went directly to the bathroom. That was so characteristic of Lu Weijun, she thought, always so straightforward, and his straightforwardness was often tinged with light-hearted vulgarities. Xiqing was just the opposite. When it comes to matters of feelings and love she liked to cover, hide, and conceal a little, leaving something unsaid on purpose for the joy of guessing the unknown. So, on this point, she felt from the bottom of her heart that she liked Xia Zheng better.

Xia Zheng was sitting in a Manhattan coffee shop facing the street. He ordered a double cream latte. Sitting by the window, he took out his notebook computer with the intention of reselecting the pictures of his oil paintings while waiting for the person he had an appointment with to show up. You should not go under thirty thousand US dollars! Those were the words of Wang Yao. He was in New York this time for a group exhibition with several young and middle-aged painters, and Wang Yao was the general manager for the Chinese side. Today, an Italian collector in the United States wished to take a look at Xia Zheng's works with the possibility of buying some of them. As an agent, Wang Yao was supposed to be here with him, but it just so happened that a counselor of the Chinese diplomatic service had asked him for a private meeting today. Before they went their separate ways, he specifically reminded Xia Zheng that there was a figure, a bottom line that he should never go below. If the price went lower it would not be fair to those who had bought his paintings before. OK, thirty thousand US dollars. Xia Zheng was lost in his thoughts. From college days to graduation, from assuming the university teaching job to becoming artistic director of an advertising agency, from being artistic director to becoming a professional artist, Xia Zheng felt that the last decade or so seemed like a series of lines. Once he went over one line it would mean that he made a little progress, but another line would soon appear. The lines were the prices his works could fetch, and as the price was getting higher and higher, he worked less and less. At first, he wanted to paint but was stopped by Wang Yao, his logic being that productivity actually worked against his own interest. Once you made your name and too many of your works were on the market, it would be hard for you to further up your market value. Later on, he wanted to paint but he found that he no longer had full command of his art. He thought at first that holding back a little early in his career would last him longer, little did he know that gift and inspiration, like moistened seeds, if they didn't sprout once they were in the ground they would simply get mushy and rot, spoiling the soil as well. Sometimes, as his mind went through these things the thought of blaming Wang Yao would creep up, but on second thought, Wang Yao deserved most of the credit for the continued climb of the commanding price of his paintings in the last years, from hundreds of RMB to tens of thousands of US dollars. Indeed, Xia Zheng was the painter, but what would the name of Xia Zheng fetch without Wang Yao?

In the last couple of years as the artistic calling in him was diminishing, Xia Zheng also found himself in an increasingly lousy mood. He started sighing a lot. He would sit on his rattan chaise; smoke a pipe with his eyes staring in the emptiness and sigh. Even he himself was at a loss of what his sighing meant. All he knew was that he always felt that something was pressed hard against his chest. Sigh. But the sound of sighing definitely got on Xiqing's nerves. The minute she heard it she would get angry. They sometimes got into a fight and lost their temper just because of a sigh. Xiqing claimed that there was sadness in the sighs of others. "But how come yours sound so dejected? Its repetition can merely get on one's nerves!" In the last year or two her tempers seemed to have changed for the worse as well, a change that has caused him to put on hold his intention of marrying her. They have been living together for ten years, if anyone is counting. Ten years ago, also when winter was approaching, Xiqing had a bottle of red wine hidden in her bag and timidly knocked on his dormitory door.

Xia Zheng opened up the notebook in front of him, but instead of rearranging his pictures he moved the cursor to Skype when he saw the icon. He suddenly had the urge to talk to Xiqing on Skype. But he tried for a long time and there was no answer. He has been in New York for a week. On the first few days he had been busy with the exhibition and in adjusting to the time difference. Days just flew past him so fast. After the exhibition he had been busy with interviews. Today was the first time he had a half day to himself and he finally discovered that he hadn't called back home even once, and Xiqing hadn't bothered to call him up either. He looked at his watch. It should be seven o'clock in the morning over there. Today was Saturday. Xiqing was probably still asleep. Near the end of the semester all the homework for optional courses should be turned in by now, and she always spent serious time in grading students' homework.

Returning from the place of Lu Weijun, Xiqing took another shower, threw her clothes in the washer, added disinfectant, and washed her hair twice. The hot water heater had been in use for years. Its aging tubes made the water coming out of the shower head only intermittently hot. Every time she shuddered she would miss terribly the hot to the touch body of Lu Weijun. When they made love, the kisses of Lu Weijun came down like droplets of water from a watering can, splashing over every inch of her body, a little itchy, but very satisfying. But droplets needed to be wiped dry sooner or later, or one might catch cold by walking out while dripping wet. With a towel wrapping up her hair and in a bathrobe she went to her desk with the intention of calling the landlord, demanding a new water heater and new tubing. She saw Skype on her computer showed unanswered phone calls from Xia Zheng. So while wiping her hair dry, she tried to call him back. The screen misted up. The system showed that the other party was not on line. She then glanced at the date shown on the lower right hand corner: November the 11th. Bachelor's Day.

Ten years ago, when most of the people had no idea what that day was, Xiqing, who only began to know the taste of love, started feeling the loneliness of being alone. She was still in school at the time, in her early twenties, and whenever she saw someone she liked she would still blush out of timidity. On this day ten years ago she brought herself and a bottle of red wine to Xia Zheng. But men like Xia Zheng were unlikely to remember the date. He was never good with numbers.

Xiqing took off the bathrobe, started putting lotion on in front of the mirror. She liked to look at herself in the mirror, including her hair, face, neck, shoulders, breasts, waist, buttocks, and legs. Her hair had grown, so long now, if not for the poem of Wu Zuo, she would only remember herself having hair reaching to her ear lobes. It was an almond flavored lotion with a tad of bitter taste to it. Xiqing felt that the flavor fit Xia Zheng just right, once you poured it all over your skin, it would be absorbed pretty fast, any sensation of coldness would disappear once you rubbed it in a few times with both hands. Therefore, lotion was different from water, because water would eventually evaporate, it would either take away some warmth of the body or leave some stains behind, causing harm; whereas lotion would be absorbed and wouldn't cause any harm. Xiqing as reflected in the mirror might not qualify to be called a beauty, but was good-looking, as the good in "a good wife and a loving mother." If you ask one hundred men, ninety-nine of them would say that they felt comfortable having such a wife at home, a wife who was considerate, understanding, and who you never need to worry about her having extramarital affairs.

But Lu Weijun proved to be the only exception in the one hundred men.

Luka was a neutered Yorkshire dog at about four years of age. It was the dog left behind by Lu Weijun's former girlfriend Kaka. Kaka was now in the United States. After finishing two years of study she had found a position as assistant to the general manager in New York and had joined the ranks of Manhattan office workers. As for art, she told Lu Weijun, it should take the back seat for a while.

Kaka was the college roommate of Xiqing, and when Kaka noticed that Lu Weijun was in hot pursuit of Xiqing she even helped him out by passing several love letters and sketches to her. But on matters of love, Xiqing had always been equivocal. She accepted her ardent pursuer's every move without any response.

Lu Weijun and Kaka were all fine art majors, but he insisted that before meeting Xiqing in person he had had many encounters with her already, all in his dreams! He even went so far as to produce some of his sketches for Kaka as proof. Indeed, Xiqing was the girl he portrayed in all his drawings. They showed only her face, some frontal, some in profile, some looking up, and some looking down. They were portraits from all angles, and the timeline inscriptions all dated before he first met Xiqing.

You are not playing tricks on us, are you? Tilting her head, Kaka quickly glanced at Lu Weijun in disbelief.

I swear!

Lu Weijun at the time had a neatly shaved head. He seriously put three fingers against his temple, an expression of laughable sincerity on his face. Kaka recollected later that she probably started liking this boy from that moment on. She chose to believe in his words too, although Xiqing refused to believe him or his claim.

Now, every time Lu Weijun saw Luka he would think of Kaka, and he finally realized how smart this girl was. If she left some objects with him, they could be put away or thrown out, but what she left behind was a living creature! Again it was different from leaving a child behind after divorce, because a dog didn't need that much care and responsibility.

Kaka knew that if she asked for too much care from Lu Weijun, he would certainly get tired and impatient, but if she asked for nothing at all, he would feel that she had no residual value any more. But more importantly, Lu Weijun would often feel lonely and Luka would serve as his faithful companion.

That was the reason why sometimes Lu Weijun thought Kaka as the one who best understood him.

After Xiqing left, Lu Weijun went back to sleep again. Luka also obligingly took a nap curling up near his feet. In the past, he often dreamt of Xiqing, but the strange thing was that ever since they made love three years ago, she never appeared in his dreams again, and it was Kaka's turn now; once, twice, three times, she was in his dream sweetly smiling at him. Now, he and Kaka occasionally would call each other via Skype and often have phone sex. Lu Weijun believed that was the chief reason why Kaka frequently made her way into his dreams.

In the past three years every time Xiqing came to see Lu Weijun she would bring a bottle of Italian red wine. The Piemonte red wine was in fact the only wine she liked. Once Xia Zheng was invited to hold an art exhibition in Italy, Xiqing went along as his assistant, and after the exhibition she dragged Xia Zheng for an out of the way visit to Piemonte and brought back a lot of excellent wines. She herself didn't understand why she was so fascinated by red wine, but when she stood on the slope in front of the acres upon acres of grape vines, she just teared up. She was overwhelmed by the smell of this turbulent and spicy sea of red.

After dialing several times the long Skype numbers, the man Xia Zheng had been waiting for arrived. He was a Caucasian in his seventies with limited English, so he had with him a young Asian woman also serving as his interpreter. Xia Zheng thought the woman looked familiar, but he couldn't exactly recall when or where they had met. He was a little lost. He realized when everybody was seated that he hadn't had the selected pictures ready. Flustered, he immediately logged off the internet, turned off the Skype, and hastily opened a file and dragged out a few pictures on the spot.

The meeting went smoothly. The old man's name was Dino Fabou, descendant of an Italian family famous for handmade shoes. Because of his love for art collection, he had opened a creative art consulting firm in New York, thus continuing the family's inherited extraordinary sense and control on matters of esthetics and wealth. The Asian female who turned out to be Chinese was his assistant. According to her translation, the old man felt that it was time for him to pour his money into the contemporary art market of China in the next one or two years.

While walking back on Sixth Avenue, Xia Zheng was full of thoughts of the woman he just met. To be honest, he was't really that interested in what Dino Fabou said. Maybe because in recent years he had long got used to "hide" behind Wang Yao and nod, and interject only occasionally on matters of interest to him, and he didn't really know how to deal with the men in art business directly.

Xia Zheng was searching hard in his memory for a portrait to fit that woman. She wore her black hair straight with bangs. She had dark skin, pencil-thin eyebrows under which were a pair of seductive eyes. She was wearing a v-neck sea blue sweater, exposing a small part of her breast, also of a darker skin color, as to what it was like further down. Xia Zheng being polite had kept his curiosity in check. Her hands were bony. There was a clear scar on her left wrist that seemed quite deep. She used a lot of hand gestures in her talking, waving her hands back and forth, and laughing with abandon. The sound of her laugh also seemed familiar.

It was completely dark now. In the designated area the Brazilian vendors were already setting up shops one after another. They usually didn't hawk, just sat at their shops silently or with each other in two or three and chatted. Behind them the lighted skyscrapers seemed like a huge poster, when lights seemed to have moved in the autumn breeze everything became hazy and unreal. This was the second time Xia Zheng visited the United States, his last visit was ten years ago when he came for a seminar as a member of the school exchange program. "West as an Engine in Promoting the Chinese Contemporary Art Market" was the theme of that seminar. Ten years just went by in the blink of an eye.

2

When the class of Art Psychology was over Xiqing finally got a good look at an art student named Lu Weijun in the corridor of the Building of Fine Arts and History. His head was shaven clean. He had on a colorful sweater, a pair of black flannel sports pants, and a pair of dirty white-turned-grey sneakers. Xiqing didn't stand there and watch. She just got it all by way of a quick glance. Lu Weijun wasn't there to see her either. He was there for the purpose of being seen. He had a sketch board under his armpit and was crossing the building corridor on his way to the studio.

Kaka had passed those sketches of Lu Weijun to Xiqing many times. She only took a brief look at them, put them away in a case underneath her bed that collected assorted things, and never mentioned them again. It was Xiqing's sophomore year when fake pearl earrings that started appearing on her ear lobes and the ear-length pageboy hairstyle gave her a look of a girl school student of the 1930s. Her hometown was Panyu in Guangdong Province, very close to where the "Little Devil Xu" (nickname of Xu Guangping, the wife of the very famous Chinese writer Lu Xun) came from. She started reading *Letters between Two Places* (by Lu Xun and Xu Guangping) when still in high school and almost knew it by heart. She sometimes hid the book inside the comforter. Her heartbeat would begin to race and she would get hot flashes every time she thought of the emotional tussle beneath the wooden-like words and phrases, but she had no one to confess to. Her sister Zhuqing, who was five years her senior, should have been an ideal person for girl-talk, but she found out she was pregnant right after graduating from junior high school, so she got married and was now the mother of a boy of nine. She didn't have a job to go to, so she sat in the yard under the sun all day, knitting sweaters for her son and husband. In the eyes of Xiqing, there was a huge gap between Zhuqing at her present state and herself. Zhuqing was no longer the sister with whom she fought for the blanket, played tickling games or shared girlie talks with like in the old days.

When Xiqing left home to study in another town, Zhuqing also went to the train station with her son to see her off. Xiqing misted the window glass that kept them apart. It was a game they used to play when they were young. She still found it hard to let go of her sister at a time like this. But Zhuqing didn't seem to have noticed because her son suddenly broke free of her hold and ran towards the end of the train chortling. She had no choice but to go after him. Looking at the back of her sister she noticed that she had gained weight, and she had fat to spare around her waist. The dark brown dress with long sleeves that she had on was the wrong size and the wrong outfit on a hot day like this. Her hair was newly permed, like a newly blossomed chrysanthemum. In her stupor she seemed to see another Zhuqing not far from here. It was spring and she was in her last year of the three year junior high school, sporting a thick ponytail, tall, and full figured with a tight and compact built. She was wearing a sleeveless dress in light blue with an umbrella in hand as if she was waiting for Xiqing for their walk home together after school. The days were hard then. They had only one umbrella for kids. Every time it rained Zhuqing would take her to school first, meet her after school, and they'd walk back home together. But now things were different. Zhuqing married Wu Yue, the owner of a private winery. Ever since they had a rich in-law of the Wu family, they became a moderately prosperous family in Panyu as well. The only regret for Xiqing was that when they had almost everything they wanted, Zhuqing was no longer who she once was.

When the steam whistle sounded the first time, Xiqing turned her head away from her parents, away from her sister. She felt a hard-pressed pain that surged up along her esophagus. Her face became numb. She must look terrible. But it was exactly then that she heard three thumps on the car window. It was Zhuqing. Beads of sweat could be seen on her forehead. Her face was also flushed red. She held the wrist of her mischievous boy firmly in hand and smiled at Xiqing, baring two naughty canines. She drew her head close to the window pane and also misted the glass. The pain hesitating at Xiqing's throat thus went immediately to her sinus and retina.

Her mouth opened up and she cried a heartbreaking cry. But Zhuqing broke into a smile, a natural and gentle smile. She stood in place, patted on the head of her son as if she was comforting Xiqing, be nice, don't cry.

Tears always seemed to well up in her eyes throughout the train ride. They stayed wet and moist as if they were misted by Zhuqing and refused to be wiped away.

Kaka had really been annoyed by Xiqing's attitude towards Lu Weijun. She didn't care for Lu Weijun at first, but then she felt that Xiqing needed to take a stance, for or against, and her ambiguity really didn't sit well with Kaka. She had accepted so many sketches and had seen him more than once, and yet she gave no sign whether she found him to her liking or not. As days dragged into months, Lu Weijun used so many excuses to dine, chat, and study with Kaka, as if they were the ones who actually had endless things to talk about. In fact, all Lu Weijun wanted was to find out from Kaka what Xiqing thought of him. The truth was that Kaka had no secret information to share with him. She sometimes just turned around and walked away when his pestering got on her nerves. Like a child who knew that he was in the wrong, Lu

Weijun would then follow closely behind her and ask
for forgiveness. In the end, the two of them were seen
as going steady in the eyes of others.

Deep inside Kaka felt that her roommate Xiqing,
with whom she now and then did things together,
was like cold water in the pond. She wrapped herself
carefully in layers. No one really knew, nor was anyone
ever to know how deep the water was and what was
hidden inside.

Once, Kaka promised Lu Weijun to persuade
Xiqing to attend an open class of art history offered by
the Art Department, so as to give him an opportunity
to strike up a real conversation with Xiqing. But when
the class was over, Xiqing acted as if she was under a
trance and her soul had left her body. She left without
saying a word to anyone, leaving Kaka and Lu Weijun
stunned on the spot. When Kaka asked Xiqing what
had happened after returning to their dorm, her terse
reply was: nothing was the matter. Her feelings hurt,
Kaka then told Lu Weijun that from then on he was
on his own as far as Xiqing was concerned and that
she had no intention or interest in getting herself
involved anymore.

Before going to the class Xiqing already heard about
Xia Zheng. He was considered somewhat famous

in school. His open class had been very popular, so Xiqing arrived early and got two seats in the middle towards the front. She also had a book with her, in case the lecture was under par she would have something to pass her time with. Kaka on the other hand started looking around the minute she sat down, wondering how come Lu Weijun hadn't showed up.

Students started arriving in the classroom. Girls mostly came in groups of three or five. They wore different hairstyles, brimming with youthful radiance, whereas the boys just loved to be their independent selves. As usual, Lu Weijun with a notepad under his armpit and a pen in his mouth slipped inside the classroom quick as a whirlwind. His outfit was basically the same as the one Xiqing saw him wore in the corridor of the Fine Arts and History building, except that this time he had a gray knitting cap on his shaved head, completely covering his ears and down to his eyebrows. Some of the girls started heckling. Hey, Lu Weijun, didn't you know that spring is here? Lu Weijun shrugged. It's none of your business. He plumped on a desk in the first row with his legs far apart, circled three times, and finally settled in a row right in front of Xiqing. The day before yesterday he had a little too much to drink and got into a fight. The back of his head was hit by a beer bottle and sustained a cut that required three stitches. It wasn't that serious of a wound, but the shards also nicked his left ear in several places and the scars only began to form. In the dorm, Lu Weijun took a side view in the mirror and decided to wear a cap to cover his embarrassment. After all, it was today that he would like to have a few words with the girl of his dreams, Xu Xiqing.

Right after settling down, he started pondering on how to say hello to Kaka and the other girl in the back first. But right at that moment Xia Zheng walked into the room in measured steps, so he only had time to turn his head and make a face at Kaka and take a quick glance at Xiqing in passing. Xiqing was totally absorbed in her reading. She had on a light purple crew neck sweater, baring her snow white collarbones.

The noisy classroom gradually quieted down, as if the fire underneath the boiling water had just been turned off. Xiqing also sensed the change and closed the book before her, raised her eyes to look at Xia Zheng, and also at the back of the head of Lu Weijun in passing. She was actually aware of the glimpse Lu Weijun threw at her when he turned his head just now.

While in high school in her hometown, a boy once

also revealed his feelings for her. The boy copied a poem *The Reeds and Rushes* from the *Classic of Poetry*, inserted it in his weekly report notebook and gave it to Xiqing in secret. In it there was also a picture of her, but she had no idea when it was taken. The boy was a class representative despised by her classmates for being a tattletale, so his confession actually frightened Xiqing. She was afraid of being isolated by the others because of this poem. She stuffed the notebook in the back of her desk drawer and tried to press it in even further every time she put her book bag in there. A week passed and nothing happened, then one day after school the boy appeared suddenly before Xiqing without an excuse and said: Give me back my notebook. At the time, Xiqing felt that her heart was about to jump out from her throat. She used her hand to dig out the notebook in her desk drawer, but it was pressed so hard by her book bag that she couldn't get it out. She tried once, twice, but she was so anxious that sweat started forming on her forehead. She was on the verge of tears from embarrassment. Then finally the notebook came out. It was all wrinkled up. One corner of the blue cover was folded over, bearing the white piece of paper with the poem *The Reeds and Rushes* on it. He grabbed the notebook with full force, maybe because he was too nervous, and left without turning back. Afterwards, rumor started to fly among her classmates about Xiqing and this boy, but in time it died a natural death for lack of any follow-up development. Nowadays, when recalling that episode, aside from the embarrassment of her heart about to jump out of her throat, she only remembered the badly wrinkled blue notebook and the paper the poem appeared on that looked so white in contrast.

Towards the end of the class, Xia Zheng informed the students that four weeks from now there would be no class for two weeks.

I have to attend a meeting in the United States, so class will be suspended for two weeks.

After these words, he turned and erased what he wrote on the blackboard, a habit he formed after becoming a teacher. He didn't expect the college kids to keep doing the chores of students on duty like in their earlier student days, and he had no intention of leaving the work for the professor who came to use the classroom next either. He was in a rather good mood today. He noticed Xiqing at the beginning of the class. To be exact, Lu Weijun was the one who caught his attention first as he was the only one wearing a hat in the classroom. The students in the first few rows were all art majors. There were about thirty of them whom he knew very well. But there was a newcomer sitting right behind Lu Weijun. She had listened attentively to the one and a half hour lecture and was never distracted throughout by the book that was open before her.

Xia Zheng realized after becoming a teacher that no matter how big the classroom or the student body, once you stepped on the platform that stands above the ground you would have a commanding view of whatever happened in the room. There were students dozing off, passing notes, playing with their cellphones or daydreaming. He could see everything clearly. Usually he would have two hours of material prepared for the hour and a half lecture. He also enjoyed lecturing while appreciating the "scenery," which was a real collection of expressions: the furtive look, the scary look, the exhausted look, the excited look, the look of striking a chord, the blasé look. They intermingled to form a scroll painting with no end.

In today's one and a half hour Xia Zheng spent most of the time sizing up Xiqing. He felt that she was good-looking, and yet it was really hard to pinpoint the source of her good looks. Her features? Her hair? Her skin tone? Her figure? He didn't know, just that this female student was demure and pleasant to look at. Her eyes, like water in the pond, every blink would cause a ripple. They stayed with his every move. She never engaged in private conversations with those sitting nearby and stayed silent for the whole one and half hour. She just sat there in total concentration, listening and keeping her eyes on him. In the end Xia Zheng even felt that she had said so much with her eyes, and to him. But what exactly did she say? So he himself became the most distracted one in his class.

During the whole time, Xiqing had been sizing up Xia Zheng as well. His hair was not at all flashy. With freshly trimmed sideburns, he had gentle features fit for a good teacher. He had on a dark khaki trench coat with a lemon yellow shirt underneath. He didn't wear a tie and had left the collar open, exposing his Adam's apple. His lecture was lightly punctured by his hand holding the chalk. He wrote quickly and his handwriting was beautiful, robust, and free-flowing. When he double-checked his notes he seemed a bit lost, knitting his eyebrows as if he was mulling over something. While watching him, the book *Letters between Two Places* flashed through her mind. Hmm, yes, this must be the way the "she" in the book had been staring at the person standing on the platform.

After one and a half hour of quiet observation,

Xiqing completely forgot about the existence of Lu
Weijun sitting in front of her, or Kaka sitting next to
her, or the existence of the rest of the students in the
classroom. She was very much in a different world, a
world with just the person on the platform and her,
the only audience, a scene she read so many times
before. She had had many male teachers before, and
yet only today she seemed to have been knocked
unconscious and went in hiding in a world of her own
creation, never wishing to come out from it again.
She became tired of watching and rested her chin in
her hand for support, her eyes became moistened and
she could feel the warmth in her heart. She heard him
moving from Japanese painting to Korean ancient
sketches, the changing of slides and the flow of Xia
Zheng's cadenced language meant that this lesson
on contemporary history of East Asian painting was
slowly coming to an end. Xiqing listened carefully.
Every sentence seemed to have come in as a tap on
her head, but it then surreptitiously escaped from the
other ear, leaving her with nothing but a warm sense
of bliss. She only slowly regained her senses when
Xia Zheng announced that the class was dismissed
and turned to erase the board clean. Kaka who sat
next to her did an exaggerated body stretch, Xiqing
felt that she had been in a long dream, and now the

other world just disappeared without a trace. Staring at the back of Xia Zheng walking away, she was hit by a sudden sense of sadness and felt like crying.

How do you do, Xu Xiqing? My name is Lu Weijun. I am also from Guangdong. I did many sketches of you.

Lu Weijun finally opened up. His mind was somewhere else throughout the class. He had run through so many different versions of self-introduction. Have they had any conversation in dreams? Probably not. He remembered the first time he set eyes on Xiqing. It was exactly the same scene occurred repeatedly in his dreams; a girl walking towards him against the golden sunset, a lithe and graceful figure with a hint of timidity in her expression, and a sense of demureness and hesitancy in her eyes. Only that the one in his dream was more like cotton puffs, they crumbled in hands, but when he tried to kiss her the response was ardent, so incongruous with her looks, but her hands were cold. When they slipped down his chest he would be left with a sense of numbness as if he was hit by lightning. So every morning he woke up with his sheet stained by his wet dreams. Sometimes, the woman would disappear from his dream for a whole month. He would then become anxious, appear absent-minded in class and doodled time and again the woman on paper. He was told that if he saw her often enough during the day, she would surely show up in his dream, so she appeared in numerous of his sketches, in all expressions and postures, and he became the best sketch artist in school.

Lu Weijun lost his parents early in life and was reared by his maternal grandmother until he was thirteen when she passed away. It was then arranged to have him live with the family of his aunt in Panyu. His aunt had a son about the same age as Lu Weijun, but he was strange and kept to himself. Lu Weijun was afraid that his cousin would notice the semen stain on his sheet, so he got up very early every day, wiped the sheet with wet towel and used his aunt's hair dryer without her knowledge to blow it dry until the sheet hardened up. Fortunately, he passed the entrance exam to the high school in the city of Guangzhou not long afterwards and moved to live in the school dormitory.

Now in the lecture theater, the Xiqing in front of Lu Weijun still looked a bit dazed. This was the first time he looked at her up close. The silhouette of the woman in his dream was blurry, hidden behind the gauze of dream, but her expressions and body were vivid, lively, and responsive. The Xiqing in front of him was just the opposite. The silhouette was clear, but aside from that everything else seemed unfamiliar and blurry to Lu Weijun. He felt that it was possible that things became out of focus because he had problems with his vision, anyway, her expressions were as blurry as if she was several miles away even at such a close range.

Seeing that Xiqing seemed lost in her thoughts, Kaka straightened up, poked her at the arms. Hey. She had been assiduously taking notes throughout the class. She found the occasional sight of Lu Weijun sitting in front fidgeting in his seat or scratching his woolen knit cap amusing. She knew that Lu Weijun must be nervous as hell. She saw that the hat moved a little as a result of his scratching and a bloody scar on the exposed part of his ear came into view. He must be a ferocious fighter. When Kaka was small, her father had been in charge of discipline in school. Kids like Lu Weijun with the "potential" to go astray had been the subjects of his concern, but she against all odds, had a special weakness for kids like that. So long as they were not the kind who only dared to challenge the weak, being a little rude and rakish would only add to their cuteness.

Xiqing only regained her presence of mind after

a long while. She couldn't help but take another look
at Xia Zheng who just collected his notes and was
walking slowly out of the classroom. His steps were
light and measured. As she collected her thoughts, the
image of Lu Weijun standing in front of her became
extra clear. It was a close-up of his face. His shaved
head wearing a knit cap looked like an egg with a dark
colored shell. Xiqing was a little uptight, at a loss of
what to say, with a nervous smile she started also to
collect her belongings. She wanted to leave this place
fast. She seemed to have slept deeply during the one
and a half hour class, and when she suddenly woke up
everything around her seemed to have changed and
looked strange.

When walking out of the classroom Xia Zheng
wanted so much to look back again. He turned his
back and started clearing the blackboard right after the
class was over. When he finished clearing and turned
around he couldn't see her anymore, because she was
totally blocked by the male student with a knit cap.
He lingered there for a while, wishing that he could
approach them and say something. After all he was
the teacher and he could very well ask them how they
found his class and whether they need any further
clarifications. He could perhaps then ask naturally for

her name. He was only curious about whom she was and he had a favorable impression of her, but in the end nothing happened. He felt that such an approach might be too intrusive. The truth was that he never took the initiative of striking a conversation with students unless they came up to him with questions. He was also aware of the fact that most of the female students who asked him questions merely wanted to talk to him. He was so used to it beginning from his school days to being a teacher. He had been a draw for girls. They found him attractive because he was a great painter, a great calligrapher, and someone with reasonably good looks. But it just happened that no one came to him for questions after class today. Wouldn't it be nice if he was detained, even for a little while, by a question popped up by someone? That was the thought that crossed his mind.

3

When Xia Zheng returned to the hotel Wang Yao was sipping coffee in the lounge. Spotting Xia Zheng from afar, he called out his name and greeted him with waving arms. Xia Zheng! Next to Wang Yao, he saw the Asian girl he met a while ago. She sat there

relaxed and only rose up when he was in front of her.
How do you do, Teacher Xia. While Xia Zheng was
still somewhat confused, unable to decipher what was
going on, Wang Yao broke out laughing. My, my, Xia
Zheng, I was told that you didn't recognize her just
now! The Asian lady also responded with a big smile,
her teeth were gleamingly white.

Xia Zheng examined her carefully. The face
still looked familiar. He was about to remember
where they met before when a sudden gust of wind
blew all his clues into thin air. He felt that recently
his memory, as everything else about him, had been
failing. As she was standing up she seemed tall. She
was wearing a bright red silky ski outfit over a sea
blue sweater. Her complexion seemed rosier than it
was in the afternoon, though tiredness could easily be
detected from her eyes. But who was she?

My name is Bi Lu, also known as Kaka, college
roommate of Xiqing, Arts major, class of 96. Xia
Zheng, Teacher Xia. Seeing that Xia Zheng after such
a long time still couldn't recall who she was, Kaka
refused to play this game any longer. Xia Zheng had
apparently aged, his senses slowed. In the afternoon
she had spotted him sitting there from afar, wearing
an old-styled khaki-colored trench coat over a dark

blue shirt. Bathing in the golden sunshine that cast directly on his face through the window pane, he somehow cut a lonesome figure. He seemed to have stared at his computer for a long while, leaving the coffee untouched, the foam already sank to the bottom. Only the silky ripples remained on the surface. She followed Dino Fabou in approaching him and greeted him in Chinese. It was only then that he stood up stiffly. What followed was a flurry of panic moves. With the intention of getting him back on track, Kaka took control of the pace of the meeting, thus allowing him sufficient time to introduce himself. She knew that Dino Fabou was not an easy negotiator. He had dealt with as many artists as the number of women he laid.

Wang Yao waved for the waiter to bring him a menu. So where did you go after that? He asked.

Xia Zheng shook his head. I just walked around. I want a glass of water. He finally remembered who Kaka was. Still, he felt terrible. Bi Lu must be a name he often heard of ten years ago, because she was the roommate of Xiqing and also because he sometimes ran into them when browsing at the Manglu (Galloping Deer) Bookstore. But what was truly alarming was that he had almost erased this person from his memory now, and he didn't know how many more once important persons or events had also been so unceremoniously erased by the passing of time. He didn't remember anymore. Was he misleading himself or was he himself being misled?

Dino Fabou is a smart guy. Kaka held her neck back a little when she said that. Her face was almost totally buried in the collar of her ski jacket. Her chin against her chest, she pursed her lips.

With you helping out I don't think there will be a problem. I also have some new works by several other new artists. They too are available for talks if he is interested. Wang Yao lit a cigarette and added: You are a close friend of the wife of Xia Zheng after all. Everything else is negotiable.

Oh? They are married? This seemed to be the subject that truly aroused the interest of Kaka. She raised her chin, sat up in her seat, and signaled for a cigarette. Wang Yao immediately opened up the pack and handed it to her. No, but it's a matter of time now. Kaka choked on her first smoke, coughed a little, and looked at Xia Zheng with a furtive smile. Xiqing really harbors a long lasting love for you.

Listening to their light-hearted talk back and forth about his private life, Xia Zheng found it a bit distasteful. Remembering that no one answered the phone when he called Xiqing in the afternoon, he wanted to go back to his room and give it another try. She should be up by now. She seemed to have been down with a cold before his trip overseas. Was she better now? Living together all these years, their feelings for each other had turned into a habit, the habit of having somebody around, but only a habit. Sometimes, Xia Zheng would also seriously consider the importance of love. When he was young he had high ideals about love. During his school days he once fell for a student in a senior class who looked like Lin Qingxia (also known as Brigitte Lin, a famous Chinese movie star from Taiwan). She used to have her large size white cotton shirt stuffed in her oversized blue jeans. Still, she seemed very sexy then. The exaggerated curve of her buttocks was always a sight of excitement for male students walking behind her. Later on, he also fell for several other women a few years his senior, without exception they all had about them the scent of breast milk, a sign of maturity. But after his thirtieth birthday, Xia Zheng started feeling attracted by the qualities young girls possess; youth, fearlessness, and the seemingly inexhaustible energy and exuberance. It was from then on that he became confused about what love was. Then he met Xiqing, someone who made his heart flutter at first sight. At the very beginning, they had experienced hesitations, exaltations, misgivings, and longing, as if it was a long phase of foreplay, leading finally to a climax. In theory they should be satisfied, ready to nestle against each other and stay together forever. But how did they end up? Looking back at the ten years they were together, he ended up thinking that it was an unremarkable ten years.

I will go back to my room if you don't mind, I have some business to attend to, you two can take your time. Xia Zheng felt a little tired, he found the conversation between Wang Yao and Kaka truly uninteresting. He tried to remember the looks of the old Italian guy he met this afternoon to no avail. After returning to his room he prepared a cup of green tea for himself, standing in front of the floor to ceiling glass he was soaking in the night scene of New York. The glass misted up by the hot tea seemed wistful, the night scene outside seemed like a painting, with his face, a lifeless image, imprinted on it in two light silhouettes. He stood there lost in thoughts, lowered his head and checked the time, it was midnight. He then turned around and started calling Xiqing, not long after he clicked open the Skype window the phone went through. He immediately took out the invitation card for the show out of the pocket of his trench coat and waved it at the window. The show opened and it was a success, he said.

In the small window Xiqing was wearing a light green soft velvet housecoat, her still soggy hair rested on her breasts. Xia Zheng smiled, extended his fingers to touch her face, tips of her hair, collar bones, shoulders, and breasts on the screen. He wanted so much to go down further, but was stopped by the desk. I miss you a lot, he said. Once those words came out he himself was touched and got misty-eyed. It was a starry night for the city of New York outside, but he knew that if he turned his head and looked at it again he could only get a sense of chill. He wanted to go home.

Xiqing had some congee for lunch, so as to give her alcohol soaked stomach some rest. He then used the hair dryer to blow her hair half dry and sat in front of her desk to mark the mid-term papers handed in by students who took the class this semester. She was teaching literature to undergraduates at a technical institute. The course work was not demanding, most of the students were male, so a half full classroom was considered a good attendance. But as a course that had four credits to it, the students flocked to the class anyway, only that they mostly just wanted to muddle through by cutting and pasting something from the internet and turned it in as their homework. Xiqing didn't want to give the students a hard time, and to save them from an embarrassing low mark she would give a uniform B minus to such homework. But this semester a student named Wu Zuo just stood out. He always sat in the first row, never missed a class, and would even chime in when he got excited about the subject under discussion. In the past, Xiqing's was the only voice in class. She also didn't use the blackboard often, never posed questions to her students, and towards the end of the semester she would make public answers to exam questions in long stretches, leaving students with the words, "just try to memorize them, good luck." Having a student like Wu Zuo all of a sudden simply tired her out. Other students were happy to be onlookers, like the audience of a play with one major player and another one echoing in agreement. They even found it amusing to spread among themselves the rumor of a teacher student love affair after class. There wasn't much Xiqing could do about this unwanted attention. She just had to be more careful than before in her class preparation to prevent careless mistakes.

This time Wu Zuo turned in a new style poem entitled *You* as his free verse homework, in which every word was about Xiqing. Xiqing felt that the poem failed as it was too revealing, since she knew it was about her. Only the sentence "long tresses, like silk curtains, draped over her shoulders" reminded her that she now had long hair. In the end, she gave him an A-, with a two-word comment, "quite good." She put the homework of Wu Zuo which was on top of the pile to the other pile labeled "already marked," suddenly, the computer screen lit up again. It was Xia Zheng.

Xia Zheng appeared on the screen, wearing a khaki trench coat over a navy blue shirt, the same trench coat he had on when she saw him the first time, she remembered.

I was grading the homework until very late last night and slept until a little after ten this morning, she said. When will you be back? She also asked. They hadn't been in touch for a week. Xia Zheng was like that. He became oblivious to her existence whenever he was preoccupied with his own business. In the past that was reason enough for her to get the blues, but she felt differently now. She had a hard time in pinpointing the difference. She still loved Xia Zheng, only that her mood would no longer swing with his every move. Maybe this was a sign that she was growing up. She would stay calm as in kind wind and gentle rain even when bluffed by billowing waves. She also knew why she needed Lu Weijun, because this man had vigor that she found missing in Xia Zheng.

Yes, vigor. She liked the shock brought about by Lu Weijun's penetration into her, the seemingly unstoppable shock of a fast flying plane touching down. Every time at the advent of that moment she would grab tight the back of Lu Weijun, her fingernails pressing deeply into his flesh, until he uttered a roar from deep down his throat. She loved so much the alcohol and saliva mixed kisses and panting, the out of control accelerated heartbeat, the sinking, going down, straight down until they hit the ground, arrival, deceleration, and gradual restoration to calm. This was the kind of heartbeat that she needed.

After her phone call with Xia Zheng, Xiqing phoned Lu Weijun. Kaka ran into Xia Zheng in New York, she said. The words were meant to ask Lu Weijun to make sure that Kaka knew her place. She knew very well that everyone has someone else that he or she is afraid of. If Xiqing was the one who could keep Lu Weijun in check, then Lu Weijun was the one who could keep Kaka in check.

The voice of Lu Weijun on the other end of the line sounded as if he was still in dream. He gave only vague responses and assured Xiqing that there was no need for her to worry about anything. If she wanted to say something she would have said it three years ago. Giving a pat at Luka's behind and stretching his body a little, he added: Why did you leave in such a hurry. I really miss you.

"Get out!" With these words Xiqing hung up. Stroking her not completely dried hair, she thought of Kaka whose image three years ago or ten years ago remained fresh even today. During school days Kaka was considered the friendliest girl in the dorm room, just the opposite of Xiqing. Xiqing attributed Kaka's inborn self-confidence, optimism, vitality, and natural ease in chatting, eating or drinking with boys, calling them good naturally as her younger or older brothers, her way of befriending the girls without hiding any of her secrets or harboring any ulterior motives to her growing up in the big city. Before meeting Xia Zheng, Xiqing liked to be left alone. She would rather eat alone, go to the library alone, and study alone in the classroom. But even she couldn't completely resist Kaka's friendly gestures either, so she and Kaka did spend some times together. Going to the lecture of Xia Zheng was a case in point. Strictly speaking, Kaka was the "matchmaker" for her and Xia Zheng. Without her there would probably be no follow-up to the story. Come to think of it, these chain reactions were just as wonderful as what happened in the movie *Run Lola Run*. Everyone has his or her own life, but the life would also depend on the world of someone else. If Lola changes, others would also change accordingly, and if others change, Lola would not remain the same either.

This was also true for Xiqing and Xia Zheng.

For some time now Xiqing felt that Xia Zheng had changed. He was no longer content. The second year after they moved in together, at the repeated urging of his old classmates, Xia Zheng resigned his teaching position and became an advertisement designer for their company. At the time, only a small number of people knew how to do computer-aided design. Xia Zheng put his painting work on hold, taught himself several design software, became quite good at it, and was soon promoted to be the designer-in-chief. Xiqing, on the other hand, also went on to graduate school without a hitch. She took classes during the day and prepared late-night snacks for Xia Zheng who often had to work overnight. Xiqing was extremely considerate in those days. Sometimes when Xia Zheng was detained by his clients, she would curl up in a wool blanket and wait for him on the sofa until she fell in sleep, and would only find out at dawn that he never made it home the whole night. "Busy" was the reason Xia Zheng cited the most in those years.

Later, the ad agency was closed as a result of a sudden credit crisis of its American parent company. For the first time in his life Xia Zheng found himself unemployed. It was also at this juncture that Wang Yao came onto the scene. Of course, Xiqing believed that the change she saw in Xia Zheng would be irreversible even without Wang Yao, only that the changes might be different and he would become a different Xia Zheng. But as far as she was concerned, Teacher Xia, the gentle and confident person who calmly stood on the platform as the focus of all the students was no more.

<h1 style="text-align:center">4</h1>

Xia Zheng and Xiqing met the second time at the Manglu Bookstore. It was the day before his trip to attend the seminar in the United States. He felt that he needed some reading material on the plane and a Longman pocket dictionary just in case. The minute he walked in the store he spotted Xiqing on the far end. In a black knitted vest over a cherry red turtleneck, she was standing in front of racks of books about fine art and holding a Southeast Asia art history book with a green jacket. Xia Zheng felt a tinge of guilt because most of his prepared notes for his last class came from that book. It was warm in the store. The wife of the storeowner smiled and chatted with him as usual.

Xia Zheng put his umbrella in the lead pail. For a while he forgot why he came to the store in the first place, and moved towards Xiqing. He stopped in front of a bookshelf, got a book out in passing, and flipped through the pages. He soon felt that his body was totally enveloped in the wet warmth of the store. The wet air permeated the whole store.

A while later, Xia Zheng made his first move. He walked over to Xiqing and nonchalantly said, you were in my class, right?

Xiqing passed a sleepless night that night. She was reading a book in silence under a flashlight. There were pencil-written comments throughout. She lightly touched the written commentaries, and found the image of him preparing his lectures under a faint lamp light quietly exhilarating. In fact, she was still in a daze when she received from him the book *Southeast Asia Art History* under a sequoia tree outside the living quarters for school staff members. She didn't even remember how she followed him out of the bookstore. On their walk back she had been carefully dissecting the words he said to her a few minutes ago in front of the bookshelves. "Do you like the book? I have it, and I can lend it to you."

She felt so good just to walk beside him.

The day when Xia Zheng returned from his first trip to the United States was etched in Xiqing's memory, because half a month was such a long time for her. She started paying attention to the corridors of the Art Department where there were periodic joint exhibitions by teachers and students. She went to bookstores to collect Xia Zheng's painting albums and searched for his works in the school corridors. She looked at his painting of his mother, a stoop-backed old lady of the Miao nationality. She looked at his landscape paintings of the western Hunan province. They seemed to convey even more powerful images than Shen Congwen's novels. His Shanghai paintings had a touch of misery and desolation to them. Xia Zheng was no longer a stranger to her because his paintings had said all he wanted to say.

Half a month seemed endless because Xiqing tried in her mind to meet face to face with Xia

Zheng and carry out a conversation with him. She was able to clearly treat every detail as a process of moving forward. She knew that he grew up in a traditional Miao village and his first experience with pictures was a folk-art embroidery work by his mother. She knew that he was recommended for admission for both junior and senior high school and only came to Shanghai after he got the highest score at the local exam in the category of arts and culture. She knew that he was generally recognized as an extraordinarily talented student in the Art Department during college. She also knew about his past love life. When reminiscing this impossibly drawn-out half a month many years later Xiqing still felt that it could even outlast the length of ten years. She realized only then that the sense of no-end-in-sight conveyed a feeling deep in her heart and it had nothing to do with time.

Lu Weijun gradually came to notice Xiqing's interest in Xia Zheng. He was surprised by his first unexpected sighting of her in the Art Department corridor. The second sighting had him in quiet exhilaration, but by the time of her third appearance he already noticed her prolonged stay in front of Xia Zheng's oil painting. Actually, men also possessed the sixth sense, late in developing as it might often be the case. Although their sense might not be as acute as women, they could be more decisive when it comes to action, as long as they were pushed from behind. And what pushed Lu Weijun into a direct and hot pursuit of Xiqing was this discovery. His pursuit was no longer as simple as passing a few sketches through Kaka. He asked her out, for dinner, for movies, for a walk in the park, and for outings together with the rest of the Art Department. He told her I like you, would you like to be my girlfriend? As he was nervous, his words sounded as unpleasant as the noise of honing a saber blade. Xiqing was non-committal, merely asked him to take her back to the dormitory. As they reached the dormitory building, Kaka came into view on the terrace.

In fact, Xiqing discovered long ago that Lu Weijun made a good impression on Kaka. She never said as much because she intended to watch this show as a bystander. So what if you are a city girl, a friendly girl, didn't you just do the silly thing of pushing someone you love towards someone else? Although at the beginning she wasn't sure exactly what to think of Lu Weijun. After all being the object of such an all-out pursuit and love did satisfy the vanity she harbored inside. This vanity led her to believe that she probably liked this boy a little, but the like that only started to develop in her disappeared without a trace the first time she met Xia Zheng.

Sometimes Xiqing felt that compared to Xia Zheng, Lu Weijun was better in giving her a great time, and she could also sense his love for her and her importance for him without much trying, but the feeling was not mutual, and the more she didn't care about his feelings for her the more anxious Lu Weijun became, to the point of becoming a kind of pressure for her. So, she disclosed to Lu Weijun at an appropriate time that Kaka always liked him.

5

Watching Xia Zheng walking towards the elevator, Kaka burped a little and the fragrance of coffee filled her mouth. She felt that she was in a great mood today. She could imagine how Xiqing became tense once she knew that Kaka ran into Xia Zheng in New York. She would surely cut short her conversation with Xia Zheng at the first opportunity and call Lu Weijun.

Seeing that Xia Zheng was gone, Wang Yao moved closer to Kaka. With a hand stretching out to reach her shoulder, he wrinkled his fat face and said, I haven't seen you for three years and you are more charming than before. The thought of what happened one night three years ago still gave him a sense of rapture. Kaka skillfully averted his advance by raising her hand to signal the waitress for some ice water, then turned her head and responded. Why don't you have one too, just to cool you down a bit. Wang Yao burst out laughing at those words.

Wang Yao had a big bald head and a tuft of whiskers under his chin. His skin tone was fair and his increased waistline served as a living testimony to his age. In a crisply-pressed Chinese tunic suit, he looked quite impressive while sitting, but being vertically challenged his pants would invariably form huge bulges where they met his shoes when he stood up, as if they were two empty rice bags. Kaka found him more repulsive than he was three years ago, but she didn't wear her feelings on her sleeves. That was the change she made to herself in time, and that was why she was now an astute and smooth operator, always leaving a way out for others and never offending anyone.

If there are offers for Xia Zheng's paintings, you are going to make a lot of money, right? She lit a cigarette for herself while squinting to check her cellphone. There was a message from Dino Fabou. Missing you!

Wouldn't that depend on how you sweet-talked Dino Fabou? If the old man decided to collect Xia Zheng's painting, value of his future paintings would certainly not be the same. Wang Yao, laying his body all the way back and with both his hands extending sideways, continued. Once the sale goes through I will take care of your part of the business. You have to know that I am the only one you can trust to have it done smoothly and properly in China.

Good. Here I am giving you my thanks in advance. Kaka drank the whole glass of ice water in one gulp and felt the immense satisfaction of having the cold reaching her heart and lungs. I have to go, the old man was asking for me. With these words, she stood up and walked towards the hall entrance. She took a deep breath and sneaked into the complete darkness of the New York City night.

After Dino Fabou left, Kaka rang up Lu Weijun as usual. It was three o'clock in the afternoon in Shanghai, and not the best time for lovemaking. But she needed it. She felt that dampness was covering every inch of her skin, even her heart, and she needed to be baked dry by the voice of Lu Weijun. They made heated love through Skype, mumbling in both Chinese and English. Kaka could feel the force coming from thousands of miles away, the sensation of high she got out of spatial distance immediately calmed her down, as if her soul just left her body and became one with Lu Weijun, at a certain place, a certain point. At this very moment, she wanted to forget everything, to be totally carefree.

She gradually recovered herself in front of the computer and turned off the video streaming. With her upper body naked she picked up the mike and talked to Lu Weijun some more about nothing of importance. Lu Weijun didn't ask her about Xia Zheng, and Kaka didn't refer to that subject either. Like old friends who haven't seen each other for years, they talked about food, weather, topics related to Luka, and then they bade their goodbyes. Bye, baby. That might sound like meaningless show words, but that was really how they addressed each other in the past, to others they were a pair of happy and sweet young lovers.

After hanging up, Kaka submerged herself in a tub of warm water. She opened her eyes in an attempt to check the tub bottom. The stinging to her eyes forced her to float up like a corpse. This one-bedroom apartment on the 37th floor was purchased for her by

Dino Fabou. He had three more mistresses like her in New York City. They were not only his physical partners, but able business assistants as well. He needed them, but when the time comes he never said as much, he would only say that he "missed" someone and would wait to be "given" of what he needed like a child. But Kaka knew very well that Dino Fabou was smarter and more capable than all the men she had ever encountered. His gentlemanlike manners and kindness were merely a piece of clothing that he needed for appearing decent in front of others.

For Kaka, making love with Dino Fabou was a process with no specific end in sight. He relied on stimulant to excite his organ and once he succeeded in penetrating he would hold tight his partner and started talking sweet nonsense. He enjoyed dressing his eyes directly at Kaka from the top down, praising her beauty which was unique to the East, with soft and flirting words. Sometimes, he also liked to place himself on the back of Kaka and buried his whole face into her hair, his body shuddering out of control. His body was aging, his skin was dried into wrinkles, and their lovemaking always came to an end when the effect of the drug wore off. Kaka would get sad at the thought of this every time.

She realized that no one could win the race with

time and age, because they ran so fast.

Arranged by Kaka, Dino Fabou met with Xia Zheng one more time. Wang Yao was also present and he had carefully prepared a CD displaying the works of Xia Zheng in the last few years, with the offered price for each at auctions, and they showed that the prospect looked good and the curve was going up.

He doesn't have that many works, but every one of them fetched a good price. Wang Yao said. This was not his first meeting with Dino Fabou. When the old man travelled to China three years ago looking for a Chinese assistant, he took Kaka under his wing at the recommendation of Wang Yao. Although Dino Fabou was a well-known and recognized figure at international art auctions, he was a new comer in the contemporary Chinese art market. As such, he didn't dare to venture into this market and remained as an observer at Qingliange and Hanhai auctions, giving Kaka some exposure on the side.

Dino Fabou was very satisfied with Kaka, not only with her looks, but also with the smartness in her character. In the few years she has been in New York she was the one who worked the hardest among all his assistants, and of course, he was also satisfied with her in bed. He liked her hair, straight, jet black and shiny.

Her darker skin tone also looked nice. Unfortunately, he was old, or he might still have the passion for love. But now he had left in him only the zeal for body and lust, and the sensation of being the one calling shots at auctions. In Italy, Dino Fabou had an age-appropriate wife and three children who took care of the family business. Theirs was a calm and peaceful relationship that showed no signs of disputes or loss of feelings for each other, but he simply dreaded the sight of his wife, her stooped slow walk, wrinkled forearms, and eyes opaque and cloudy as a setting moon. It was as if time had staged a demonstration against him by telling him the changes that had taken place. Dino Fabou seemed to have seen his own reflection in his wife, a depressing sight. And yet however he disliked seeing her, the thought of leaving her never entered his head. It was also a good thing that none of the four assistants cum lovers in New York ever overstepped their boundaries. Peace in life was assured so long as they didn't meet face to face with each other. He might as well let it be or he might inadvertently start a fight among them one day for their formal status.

Lately, he was preparing to shift his main collection focus from South Africa to China. He had been waiting for this moment for quite some time and was determined to meet Lang Qiaozhi at auctions, the best known person in the Chinese art auctions market. Kaka had sorted through a lot of data about Lang Qiaozhi and prepared a catalogue of the art pieces he bought in and resold, none of them were the works of Xia Zheng, and that was why Dino Fabou had his eyes set on Xia Zheng. In his heart he knew very clearly how much information contained in the CD prepared by Wang Yao were true, how much were false, how much were half true and how much were half false. He had a rough idea without doing any detailed checking. He had dealt with dozens if not hundreds of art brokers like Wang Yao in the past thirty years, and their tactics were more or less the same. Only that given the fluid nature of the art auctions market in China, they knew how to take advantage of the loopholes. But for businessmen, interest was the lubricant for friendship. He was determined to make Xia Zheng a star and use that to fight his first battle with Lang Qiaozhi at auctions.

Xia Zheng had Wang Yao sitting between him and Dino Fabou. He felt relieved by such an arrangement, for he almost didn't need to say anything, except nodding his head or smiling whenever Wang Yao needed him to back him up. A few days ago when he met with Dino Fabou alone in the same Café,

Xia Zheng was preoccupied with figuring out Kaka's identity and where they had met before. He only noticed today that the old man who, according to legend had been a heavyweight at international auctions, seemed to have retained some naivety as a child. He was wearing a dark green cashmere cardigan and a standard British hat, holding a walnut cane in hand. He was a slow but a clear speaker, given to hearty laughs when he got excited. Occasionally he would raise his elbows and gesture in air, as if he himself should be the artist. Xia Zheng's impression of Dino Fabou was neither good nor bad. He could also tell his relationship with Kaka.

In the end, Dino Fabou and Wang Yao reached a preliminary oral agreement. He would offer an average price of US$30,000 each for all Xia Zheng's paintings shown at the exhibition, and hoped that Wang Yao would privately buy back all Xia Zheng's works on the market at no more than $32,000 each and wait for the best time to resell. Before that he would arrange to have Xia Zheng enter the NPO contemporary art competition held every four years, with the hope of using awards to improve his name recognition and the value of his painting.

At the time of parting, Wang Yao looked somewhat worried. But Mr. Fabou, I am not sure that

all his paintings can be bought back at $32,000 each.
You have to remember that the value of his paintings
has been on constant rise in China. I have no idea if
the buyers are willing to let go of them. He extended
his hand to say goodbye to Dino Fabou.

I don't think this will be a problem. It all depends
on you, Wang. It depends on whether you have the
will to do so. Dino Fabou responded with a smile,
puncturing his cane lightly on the ground in sync
with the flow of his words and his rhythm. Crow's-
feet at the corner of his eyes were clearly visible. His
response sounded as if he would let no one to second-
guess his determination. It was at that moment that
Xia Zheng saw the piercing sharpness in the eyes of
Dino Fabou. It seemed that nothing could escape
their scrutiny. Feeling somewhat apprehensive, Xia
Zheng subconsciously looked elsewhere in an effort
to divert his attention. A wind gust started outside
the Café and went through Xia Zheng's body. He
could feel a certain kind of cold was slowly spreading
out from the bottom of his heart. Cold, very cold.

Xiqing passed out the graded homework back to
her students in class and slowly started a lecture on
"letters written by celebrities." This being the topic of
both her college and graduate theses, she considered

it something she was especially good at. But she only realized how wrong she was before as she became a teacher today, a teacher who stood on the platform and lectured in class. She once was so mesmerized by the spiritual communications between teachers and students, but as her lecturing days grew into years her excitement was almost all gone by now. There were times she could hear her heartbeats when she noticed a handsome young boy in her class was staring at her, but as her palpitation continued she would find, as she turned around, that the same student was now absorbed in his cellphone, or had fallen in sleep on top of his book. The heartbeat would then return to normal and she became resigned to reality. Xiqing believed that if she had the choice again she might not choose teaching as her profession. Then maybe she would still fall in love with Xia Zheng. But there was no if in this world.

Wu Zuo approached the lectern after class, with his homework in hand, he stood there ramrod straight, pushed his glasses up a bit and said, I am going to your place tonight. Xiqing was taken aback. She stared at him stunned, didn't know how to respond, while he walked away, without turning his head even once. Gazing at his back, she let out a small sigh. Lu Weijun's call came in unexpectedly just at that moment. He asked Xiqing to have dinner with him at his place.

I am busy tonight. Xiqing sounded cold over the phone. Her words also had an air of finality to them, untouchable like a stalactite. Lu Weijun hung up in anger. He was annoyed. In recent years every time he asked her out she would always refuse, but after no communications between them for two or three months, she would happily knock on his door with a bottle of red wine. There seemed to be a psychological war going on between them, one going backward, one moving forward, and he always seemed to be the passive one. At this thought he became paralyzed in bed, feeling dejected, and was not even in the mood to continue his half-finished painting. With his rear end up in the air, Luka was sniffing hard at the turpentine on the floor, constantly sneezing.

Lu Weijun's paintings had not been doing well in recent years, even those for sale at galleries couldn't provide him with the cash he needed. Under pressure, he was forced to lower himself to work for bars, doing fresco paintings or providing paintings for hanging, in exchange for meager payment to cover his rent and living expenses. He didn't like brokers like Wang Yao, or it wouldn't become an issue in his breaking up with

Kaka and her leaving him for America by herself. He had been in touch with his old classmates, mostly by partying with them, talking about art, and falling into drunken stupor together with them. They all said that Xia Zheng's paintings were doing well now. After all, he had been in the art world ten years earlier than they did, and in the art circle, age and fame were considered of equal importance. But in the eyes of Lu Weijun Xia Zheng was nobody. He didn't think he was superior in any way. Ten years ago the girl he loved was in love with Xia Zheng and ten years later he wouldn't like to see Xiqing's choice then being validated.

6

Xiqing was standing with trepidation in front of Xia Zheng's dormitory room. She raised her hand to knock, had a change of heart, and let her hand fall down again. It was ten in the evening. Xia Zheng was back in two weeks as he had promised the students. He went back to teaching on the podium, except that now he had a pair of rimless glasses on his nose which only served to add to his scholarly qualities. Stealing a few glimpses of him from her seat in the audience,

Xiqing was full of emotion inside, and her inability to express them had rendered her numb in her seat with her hands on desk, clutching tightly the book with a green cover. A fortnight ago they didn't set a date for the book to be returned, as if they wished to keep only a tenuous tie between them.

The next day, Xia Zheng found the green book in his dormitory mailbox, along with a note with the word "thanks" in trim and elongated handwriting. He felt that the handwriting was very much the style of Xiqing the person. The wrinkled pages seemed to have gotten wet and were blown dried with a strong smell of fragrance. His penciled commentaries now looked smudgy after being soaked. He guessed that Xiqing came over last night. Maybe she knocked on his door but he missed it because he was drunk after a night out with his colleagues. Maybe she hesitated at the door and never raised her hand to knock. Or maybe she didn't hesitate at all, but simply prepared the note ahead of time, came and put the book and the note inside his mailbox, and then just left without looking back.

He remembered running into Xiqing at Manglu Bookstore. It seemed that it was he who asked her to return the book that night. You can return the book late tonight since I'm to have a drink with my colleagues. They insisted on having a welcoming back party. Those words may be interpreted in many different ways. During the two weeks he was in the United States, the image of this particular female student often came up. He had a sense of urgency, tinged with occasional hesitancy. After all, he was the teacher and she the student. But once they met face to face, he couldn't help but succumb to his playful nature and equivocated in his response, the same way he joined other boys in making inappropriate remarks in jest to their female classmates during his student days. Still, after those words came out, Xia Zheng really felt sudden warmth emanating from his heart, spreading to his chest and abdomen and further down. But those were merely his thoughts. Once he was at the dinner party and had a few drinks, he totally forgot that he asked Xiqing to return the book to his dorm until he found the book and the note in his mailbox.

Was it possible that she misunderstood? Could it be that she thought his remarks sounded a bit flippant? Xia Zheng sighed. He curled the book up, put it into his pocket, and walked towards the school. He still felt a little dizzy. He wished to provide some explanation to Xiqing, but had no idea of what to say.

As he reached the girls' dormitory building, he just happened to see Xiqing come out. She had a travel bag with her and seemed to be in a hurry.

Hey, you, wait a minute. Xia Zheng called out to her. He realized that he didn't even know her name.

Hearing Xia Zheng's voice, Xiqing stopped. Her eyes were swollen red. Standing there facing Xia Zheng, she wanted to blink but her eyes hurt, and so did her heart. Seeing her in such an agitated state, Xia Zheng was at a loss. Are you going away? He asked. Coming closer he realized that she looked deathly pale. Xiqing nodded. I have to go home for family matters.

The night before, as Xiqing came back from Xia Zheng's dormitory, Lu Weijun was standing at the entrance of her dorm, with flushed cheeks and flitting eyes thanks to the drinks he had. As he spotted her coming his way from afar, he walked over to meet her. In the eyes of Lu Weijun, the world under the street lamps was clouded in mist. The roads looked fuzzy and so did people. He felt that he was again in a dream, and the person before him should be a compassionate being, and not as icy as Xiqing who kept people at a distance.

You ... With his arm stretched around her waist,

he didn't say another word. He just wanted to hold her in his arms with all his might. He was not drunk, just a little dizzy. He saw Xia Zheng at the restaurant, but he was the one who got drunk.

Xiqing was startled by his sudden embrace, and in no time smelled the alcohol emanating from Lu Weijun's body. She didn't try to break free, nor did she respond to his advance. Maybe it was because she felt that she had been standing in front of Xia Zheng's dorm room for too long, that her walk back also seemed unusually long. A compassionate embrace like this was exactly what her cold body needed. But in no time Lu Weijun without saying a word, lowered his head to kiss her. Flashed by the light of the street lamp coming from the back of Lu Weijun's head, Xiqing as if waking up by surprise, turned her head sideways and pushed Lu Weijun away. She took three steps back and the words she had long prepared just came out all at once. Kaka likes you. I also have someone I like, but that someone is not you! As she was tense, the words sounded mechanical. Finishing her declaration she immediately ran towards her dorm, her heart was pumping so fast. She didn't dare to look back at Lu Weijun, neither did she want to. She guessed that Kaka might have witnessed the entire scene from the terrace above.

At this moment, Xiqing's recollection of what happened last night was still vividly clear. She felt that her every quickened step towards her dorm after she pushed away Lu Weijun was not meant to distance herself from the drunkard in the alcoholic stupor, but a move towards the news of the death of her sister Zhuqing. The minute she came up the stairs, the dorm supervisor came down towards her. How come you are back so late? Something has happened to your family back home.

Xia Zheng came to know Xiqing's name only when he was in line to buy the railway ticket for her. Xu Xiqing. He held her student ID with a blue jacket in hand and stood among the crowd. From time to time he would turn and look in her direction. When he realized that her eyes were also following him he felt happy. After getting the ticket, Xia Zheng walked along with Xiqing and held the travel bag for her. Like many student lovers who had to be on their separate ways during school vacations, he also stayed with her in the waiting room, accompanied her on board, and after settling her down went back and waited in silence on the platform and gazed at her across the window. He didn't ask what had happened at home. Xiqing didn't say anything either. All of a sudden,

he felt the urge to say something to her. He turned
and jumped on board. But when coming face to face
with her in the car he was again at a loss for words,
and ended up writing a series of numbers on the back
of her ticket. He opened his arms, held her by the
shoulder, lowered his head, and whispered: Be strong,
call me when you feel the need.

When the train started moving, Xiqing stared
at the series of numbers, remembering the embrace
by Lu Weijun the night before. She turned her head
again to look at the person standing on the other side
of the window. She felt that she liked the embrace
of Xia Zheng more, the embrace that was at once
reassuring and dependable. She knew that if there was
no Xia Zheng, she might fall for the hot embrace of
Lu Weijun. But that was a big if.

7

By the time Wu Zuo arrived Xiqing already had a full
course dinner prepared. She purposefully selected a
few books from the shelf and set them aside in a pile,
ready for him to take back. Wu Zuo had the typical
good student look, pale skin, average features, well-
kept hair, and wore gold-rimmed glasses. His long

fingers were especially eye-catching every time they were used to push up his glasses. He donned a spring jacket in the color of a preserved cabbage, dark-red wool vest, and he also wore a tie, as if in keeping with the seriousness of the occasion. This was the second time he came to dinner. Xia Zheng was present the first time, but since both men were not the talkative kind, aside from the questions and answers between Xiqing and Wu Zuo the only sound you could hear throughout the dinner was the noise made by chopsticks.

He's not here? Wu Zuo glanced at the open bedroom door.

He went to the United States for an exhibition. Xiqing got a full bowl of rice for Wu Zuo. Do you find the cafeteria food ok? She asked. Wu Zuo had a grown-up appearance now. He was no longer the rambunctious little boy Zhuqing chased around the platform. Xiqing became a little sentimental at the thought of her sister Zhuqing. Because of the special relationship between the two families, Wu Zuo was never allowed to return to the Xu family after the death of Zhuqing until his admission into the school where Xiqing taught. The first time she set her eyes on the grown-up Wu Zuo Xiqing felt that he was a more calm and cool-headed presence than she remembered him as a child, and not as active and energetic, as if he was a totally changed person. But she soon seemed to find the shadow of her sister in his mouth shape and his hands. Zhuqing had a mouth just like that, full and shapely like a cooked water caltrop. Her hands were also fair and slender.

In the last ten years, all Xiqing learned about Wu Zuo were gleaned indirectly from her parents on her visits home. He was doing well in school. When her mother missed her grandson, she could only wait secretly for him at the school entrance for short exchanges. The attempted murder and suicide ten years ago were like two sharp knives that had cut deep into the heart of every member of the older generation. No one was ready to let bygones be bygones.

The last time Xiqing saw her sister Zhuqing, she was lying quietly inside the coffin, her face wearing heavy makeup. Most of her skin already turned blue. Xiqing's mother cried so hard that she fainted several times at the funeral. She cried out Zhuqing's name and kept pounding at the glass coffin, refused to be taken away. Xiqing looked at her sister. Tears kept rolling down from the corners of her eyes. She lowered her body, wishing to say a few words to Zhuqing, but she choked. In the end, she misted the glass, hoping

that Zhuqing would wake up and stretch her hand to
wipe it clean. She thought of the days she had with
her sister before her marriage and the conversation
they had had before she headed for college. She asked
Zhuqing if she didn't have Wu Zuo would she still
marry Wu Yue? But Zhuqing only stroked her face
with her hands and said, there is no if in this world.
About six months after that conversation, Wu Yue
and Zhuqing both fell to the ground after drinking
wine mixed with rat poison. Wu Yue had the lucky
star and Zhuqing didn't. The coroner found many
signs of abuse on many parts of her body, and it was
concluded that this was a case of domestic violence
triggered murder suicide. Xiqing only realized then
why for many years she never saw her sister wearing
sleeveless clothes.

Can I take a look inside? Wu Zuo asked at the
bedroom door. Xiqing nodded. She then pointed at
the other room with a closed door. Go ahead, but
don't go into Xia zheng's studio. He doesn't like the
intrusion. In the bedroom, Wu Zuo saw the picture
of a younger Xiqing, together with Xia Zheng, sitting
on a lawn. It was probably taken seven or eight years
ago. On the vanity he saw another picture in black
and white, showing two sisters, one taller than the
other, both wearing flowery skirts and canvas shoes.

Wu Zuo stopped in front of the vanity, picked up the frame with the intention of wiping the dust clean, but the glass cover was clean.

That was the picture of me and your mother taken not long before her wedding. Xiqing leaned her body by the bedroom door frame and explained. Can you tell that she was pregnant with you at the time? Wu Zuo shook his head, as if talking to himself. I don't remember quite how she looked. He turned his head and asked another question. Why don't you two get married?

Xiqing was not at all prepared for the question and didn't know how to respond, so she said "let's eat" instead.

Wu Zuo and Xiqing were sitting at a long table facing each other. He knew what was on her mind.

You look just like my mother, he said. He sounded insincere. Maybe what he wanted to say was that he saw the spiritual resemblance between the two. For ten years, aside from the little memory he had as a child, he never saw any article, let alone pictures, that he could relate to his Mom. His father Wu Yue had a new wife six months afterwards, a much younger and more beautiful wife. After she gave birth to another son for the Wu family, she also became a frequent victim of domestic abuse, much like his own mother. Ever since the sharp vineyard crop reduction and the slump in the red wine business, his father, like a bomb filled with ammunition, would explode at the slightest provocation, shattering bodies and crushing bones around him.

Xiqing didn't respond. She wanted to ask more about Zhuqing's life but was afraid of hurting his feelings, so she forced herself to swallow her questions with the gulps of rice. Neither did she mention his poem. Come to think of it, perhaps it was more a writing about her sister Zhuqing.

Any girlfriend? She suddenly thought of a question that was not embarrassing but also more appropriate to her position. Wu Zuo after all was twenty years old now. But it was at this very moment that the doorbell rang.

The second she laid her hand on the door knob Xiqing knew by intuition that the one waiting outside was Lu Weijun.

Lu Weijun was holding a small bottle of 94 Great Wall. His hair was newly washed. The bangs hanging on his forehead weren't even completely dry. He saw from downstairs that there was light in the room. He knew that Xia Zheng was not yet back home, so he bought a bottle of red wine at a convenient store nearby and took the elevator up. He felt agitated in the elevator. He knew that he shouldn't come up like this, but he just couldn't keep his feelings of resentment under control. Sizing himself up at his own reflection on the metal door, he felt everything seemed so unreal and far-fetched. Xiqing today was no longer the girl ten years ago. Maybe she never was the person in his dream. Who exactly was the person in his dream then?

Yes? Xiqing opened the door. When seeing Lu Weijun outside like she expected, she glared at him. Behind her, Wu Zuo rose up from the dining table and asked, who is it?

Seeing Wu Zuo, Lu Weijun was a little surprised. He became flustered and didn't know how to answer her. He stammered. He wanted to ask who the guy was, why he was there, and why they chose to eat at home. But what right did he have to ask those questions?

Wu Zuo hazarded a guess from the stiff back of Xiqing, from the embarrassing look of Lu Weijun and the bottle of wine he clutched in his hand. He kept his mouth shut after he guessed the intention of this man's visit. He pushed his glasses up his nose bridge with his hand, sat down and resumed eating at a measured pace. Xiqing took the wine from Lu Weijun's hand and said, thanks for the wine. As she was about to close the door, she used her eyes to ask him to leave the scene quietly. She slammed the door hard, too hard, that all three people inside and outside were taken by surprise. Her action also betrayed the embarrassment she felt. Wu Zuo laid down his bowl and chopsticks and stared at her.

Lu Weijun standing outside was so provoked that he went into a rage. He banged at the door rapidly and every bang sounded as if he meant to smash the door down. Xu Xiqing, you open the door! He screamed. His screaming bounced back from the four walls in the corridor in a dull echo. Xiqing was terrified, fearing of disturbing the neighbors she immediately opened the door again. The red wine he brought with him still in his hand.

Who is he? Once inside, Lu Weijun put his hands inside the pockets of his pants, moving his mouth at his intended direction, his shoulders held high, and asked. He assumed a devil-may-care attitude on the surface, but the fire inside his chest had long risen to his throat.

Xiqing was not moving. It was a shameful situation for her and it seemed that it was already out of control. Wu Zuo at the dining table appeared exceptionally calm. He took up the rice bowl and resumed eating very slowly. He was somewhat excited, as if he was the one who was caught red-handed. But even when it comes to catching someone in an adulterous relationship, Xia Zheng should be the concerned party and not him.

Please leave. Those were the only words Xiqing could think of after a long while. She was angry. Lu Weijun seemed ludicrous however she looked at him. What was wrong with him that he should show up here and make a scene.

Those words of Xiqing simply pushed the fire in his throat up into his brain, destroying the valve that kept insanity at bay. He sniffled, his eyes became blood-shut, his hands gripped hard at the shoulders of Xiqing and screamed: I am asking you who he is, I am asking you what do you take me for! He then walked directly to Wu Zuo, took him by his collar tie, and raised him to his feet like holding a chicken.

Wu Zuo might not be as strong as Lu Weijun, but he showed no sign of being cowed. He stubbornly stared at Lu Weijun to his face.

Let go of him! He is my nephew! Xiqing grabbed at Lu Weijun's arm from behind him with all her might. Are you out of your mind? Little did she expect to see a tear smeared face under the dining room light when Lu Weijun turned around. He felt stifled and wronged. Shaking off the hand of Xiqing, he leaned at the dining table, deflated like an airless balloon. Xiqing was thrown out of balance, tripping by her own feet she fell on the floor. A dish on the table was also dragged down with her, shattering both the dish and its contents in a loud noise.

At this moment, before Xiqing could react, Wu Zuo raised his fist and hit right at Lu Weijun's face. His fist arrived so hard and fast, Lu Weijun lost his balance, staggered backwards, hit his head on the door of Xia Zheng's studio, and was out temporarily. Wu Zuo didn't stop at that. He grabbed the wine bottle and smashed it against Lu Weijun's head.

Lu Weijun felt his head spinning. Red liquid came down like a curtain in front of his eyes. He instinctively tried to hold up the curtain with his hands. It was wine. After a while he could no longer hold himself straight and fell to the ground along the door frame. The wine seemed to have turned warm and thick, streaming down his temple and cheeks. He felt that the studio door was rammed open. Xiqing was screaming while Wu Zuo stayed where he was looking astonished. The second before he lost consciousness, he saw many paintings in the studio, many of them. He didn't have time to think of anything. He still felt the sensation in his nose. He wanted to cry.

On the eve of their return, Wang Yao hosted a dinner
for Kaka and Xia Zheng at a Chinese restaurant on
Fifth Avenue. As Christmas was approaching, the
restaurant was decorated with pine branches and
wind chimes outside, adding jingling sound off and
on in the air. Chinese dishes in New York were mostly
the improved kind, dominated by Chaozhou and
Cantonese dishes, through the sauces they used. All
dishes had a sweet and sour taste to them. Kaka was
late. She wore a short black jacket and dark brown
riding boots, looking tall and full-figured. She seemed
nonchalant in her long strides toward them. Wang
Yao would like to behave like a gentleman in front
of Kaka, so he rose up and held the seat for her. He
could smell the yellow tea fragrance she was wearing.
It smelled both sweet and intoxicating.

Once seated, Kaka turned towards Xia Zheng
and asked for Xiqing's telephone number. Xia Zheng
was a little surprised by her question. Realizing that
her question was probably too abrupt, she added
immediately: How is she now? We have lost touch
for many years and I just want to chat with her about
the old times.

Oh. Xia Zheng nodded with understanding,

took out a ball pen, and wrote down two numbers for her; home phone and cell number.

In fact, Kaka was looking for Xiqing because she got no answer when she phoned Lu Weijun the other day, and when she tried again today before leaving there was still no answer, and his cellphone was also off. This had never happened before. She also had a dream the other day. She saw Luka suddenly running towards her, barking at her, licking at her heels, his tail wagging feverishly. Lu Weijun was standing not far from her, so she called out for him but he disappeared in the blink of an eye. Waking up, Kaka had an unsettling feeling and called Lu Weijun right away, but had been unable to get in touch with him since. She wanted the help of Xiqing who surely would know where Lu Weijun was.

About three years ago, Lu Weijun and Xiqing came across each other at a gallery. Kaka knew from then on that this woman could never be taken out of Lu Weijun's heart. That heart had long been crowded with Xiqing, and she had been a fool to stick her head in without thinking. By loving him, she was doomed to be squeezed and oppressed to the point of being suffocated. That was the sorrow of Kaka.

If you fall in love with someone who doesn't love you or doesn't love you as much, you are doomed to lead a life of sorrow, because you care.

Xiqing was shopping for tonics and fruits for her hospital visit to see Lu Weijun before lunch while Wu Zuo was still at the detention center when she received the call from Kaka. She was exhausted by what happened in the past few days, both Lu Weijun and Wu Zuo had seen the paintings in Xia Zheng's studio. The neighbors all knew that Lu Weijun was injured at her place. Wu Zuo, who was a normally frail-looking scholar, suddenly showed his violent side. Her head ached. Everything gave her a headache. She didn't even have her explanations ready for Xia Zheng's return.

Do you know where Lu Weijun is? Kaka went directly to her question on the phone. She disliked Xiqing, disliked her a lot. She would like to have nothing to do with this woman the rest of her life if she could, even if she once believed that they were truly close friends.

Xiqing immediately recognized the voice of Kaka, but she still hesitated for a while, weighing what to say about Lu Weijun's injury. Xiqing remembered that Kaka started distancing from her ten years ago when she and Lu Weijun began dating. She was no longer as talkative and happy as she was before. She guarded against her as if Xiqing might take Lu Weijun away any time. But the more Kaka acted that way, the more Xiqing dismissed Lu Weijun as a contender. Her vanity also grew as Kaka heightened her vigilance, up until Kaka and Lu Weijun's graduation, their leaving the school, and their clean break with her life. When she started graduate school, she found being left alone a bit strange. She started missing him a little. After all, he who had once cared so much about her would no longer be there anymore. Her meeting with Lu Weijun and Kaka three years ago at a joint youth exhibition at the "Extreme Gallery" was more like a continuation of college life. She couldn't but feel somewhat excited, especially since her days with Xia Zheng had become dull and unexciting. Everything seemed boring.

Lu Weijun was injured, but nothing serious. He is in the hospital now. Xiqing piled the tonics on the cashier's counter. In an effort to show that she was light-hearted and wasn't worried about anything, she asked, "How much?" and handed her credit card to the cashier. She then returned to her phone call. His family members are here from Guangdong, including his aunt and cousin.

Why was he injured? Kaka asked.

He got into a fight with another. Surely, you

among all people should know his temper. Xiqing answered.

Oh, then please tell him to keep his cellphone on. Thank you! She hung up right after those words.

Xiqing put her phone away and signed the receipt, writing out her name clearly and neatly. Xu Xiqing. She felt numb as she was walking out of the supermarket with the plastic bag. Nowadays she was capable of telling lies as if they were the truth. The most important skill in lying is to deceive oneself first. She thought of the three characters she wrote just now, and asked herself if she was Xu Xiqing. Am I the Xu Xiqing I once was? Why is it that everything seemed so vague and cloudy that I just can't see things clearly? She felt that she should have asked about Kaka's life in the United States, but their dialogue was so brusque and terse, there was simply no room left for niceties.

Kaka cut the phone conversation short because Dino Fabou just arrived. She took a deep breath behind the door, adjusted her emotional state, but she still greeted him only with a stiff smile. Deep inside, she was worried about Lu Weijun, since she knew that he would not turn off his cell if he sustained only minor injuries.

Dino Fabou held Kaka in his arms. He could tell that something was bothering her from her expression. But he had no intention of finding out. He laid himself on top of Kaka and showered light kisses on her shoulders. Kaka, let's go to China next Monday. He had suspected private dealings, perhaps even some transactions, between Kaka and Wang Yao, but he didn't care about what they were or what they had been. As far as Dino Fabou was concerned, Kaka was a nice companion. He expected her loyalty, but never wanted to impose himself on her or monopolize her. In his world, women were different from works of art. They needed appreciation first and foremost, whereas works of art were only related to ownership and their set value. So, if he were a decade younger he would have loved women more.

8

Xiqing felt that it was already dawn outside. She turned carefully to grope for her underwear along the edge of the bed. She saw that the bottle of the Panyu produced red wine was practically all gone. It was lying on the floor lengthwise, still emitting the smell of alcohol. She counted the pieces of her clothing carefully and slowly, until Xia Zheng woke up and started teasing her with his hands. Every time she put one on, he took it off. He then pushed her back in bed with force and they did it again. Xiqing felt a little pain. The sheet still carried the stain of her first time. She laid her face next to Xia Zheng's shoulder and neck and said nothing. She felt peaceful.

After attending Zhuqing's funeral service, her mother gave her a bottle of red wine produced by the Wu family's winery. Zhuqing before her own marriage saved this bottle especially for Xiqing for her wedding day. With Zhuqing gone, Xiqing took it with her. She held the bottle close to her with extra care throughout the train ride. It was a bottle made with the best year of Panyu grapes. When they were small Zhuqing loved to take her younger sister to view the vineyard from a vantage point up the hill, and be overwhelmed by the surging sea of red grapes. Before her return to school, Xiqing once again went up the hill, but now the acreage of the vineyard was much smaller, with a chemical plant wedged next to it and the soil was no longer as fertile. As she was looking down, the household of the Wu family came into view, a sad and desolate sight that even sunshine couldn't make its way in.

Coming back to school, Xiqing held the red

wine in her arms to look for Xia Zheng. On the train, she read a piece of interesting news from the West. It turns out that the 11th of November was celebrated as Bachelor's Day abroad. All singles, male and female, would get together for warmth before the advent of winter. She put the red wine in her handbag and walked towards the staff dormitory. This time she knocked on Xia Zheng's door without hesitation. Things just happened, as natural as the turn of water as it reached the end of the brook.

Xiqing felt the dry warmth of Xia Zheng's body. He had been very soft and gentle with her. Every move seemed to have been carefully measured. None of them went overboard. She didn't even feel that she was rudely violated the moment he penetrated her. This being her first time she felt the pain. So this is how it's supposed to be, she thought to herself.

After Xiqing told Lu Weijun the "secret" of Kaka's feeling for him, for a long while Lu Weijun and Kaka deliberately kept each other at a distance. They sat far apart in class and would not even acknowledge each other when coming face to face. Kaka was the one who mainly avoided him. At first, upon learning that Kaka liked him, Lu Weijun didn't know what to do either. Since he had almost exhausted all his energy in his feelings for and pursuit of Xiqing, he just wasn't capable of bringing himself to face Kaka's feelings for him. He would like to have an opportunity to explain himself to Kaka, so that there would not be any misunderstanding. But he found out later that he himself was probably the one who misunderstood, because Kaka showed no interest in seeing him at all. He heard from the dorm supervisor that Xiqing had moved to a rental off campus. Xiqing on the other hand had not been avoiding him. She only became evasive when asked about her new address. Lu Weijun figured it out already. He asked Xiqing if the other person was Xia Zheng. Xiqing was taken aback and asked him how he knew it. I just know.

On an Art Department sketch trip to Huangshan at the beginning of spring, Lu Weijun broke his leg. On his climb to Lotus Peak he missed a step and fell back, seeing that Kaka was right behind him he leaned towards the other side with all his might. His ankle thus came into direct contact with two large rocks on that side. He howled in pain. After a preliminary treatment at a local hospital, Lu Weijun cut his trip short and went back to school accompanied by a teacher. Lying in bed in his dorm, he had to wait for meals brought in by classmates in another dorm. He had to use a cane under his armpit for his daily chores and he could walk only very slowly. A new classmate delivered his meal on the third day. He saw Kaka when he opened the door.

Your meal. Kaka put the disposable container on the table and was ready to leave right away. Lu Weijun leaned on the bed, raised the cane, and poked her. Hey, don't go. Stay and keep me company. He could feel his heart beat so fast when he said those words. This was the first time he felt different towards Kaka. They sat face to face, and while watching Lu Weijun eat, Kaka's eyes began to well up. She had so much she wanted to say, and yet she didn't know where or how to begin.

Lu Weijun thought Kaka was not beautiful in the traditional sense. Her skin was not fair enough, none of her features were delicate, and her long black hair, her only above-average asset, was usually bundled together in the back of her head. She walked too fast and she was loud. But she did have a winning personality and was getting along with everyone just fine. At this point, he was glad he didn't naively try to "explain" things to her as he originally thought he should. After all, what did he have to explain? He only got wind of something from Xiqing, but it could very well be her excuse to disentangle herself from him.

Did you know that Xiqing moved out? Kaka

posed the question after a long silence. It seems she's now moving in with Xia Zheng, although she said her moving out was to prepare for next year's graduate school. She added before Lu Weijun had time to respond.

Lu Weijun buried himself in the meal and withheld his comments. He had suspected as much. He had spotted Xia Zheng and Xiqing eating together in the staff cafeteria. Although he didn't detect any physical intimacy between the two, their closeness was all too obvious in their expressions and mannerisms. That got him so discouraged and dejected. Their time together hadn't been that long, and yet they were already so used to each other's presence as if they were meant to be. Ever since then Lu Weijun chose to spend most of his time in the studio. He wouldn't venture out, nor would he allow himself to drink. He had had all his hurt feelings put away. After all, what could he use to fight it out with Xia Zheng?

Why are you back so early? After a long while Lu Weijun finally raised his head and changed the subject. The Art Department's trip was supposed to last for a whole month. They were to stay at an old house up the hill where it was quiet and peaceful.

Kaka started to say something but stopped herself. She wanted to leave something for Lu Weijun to figure out. At Lotus Peak she screamed when she saw Lu Weijun fall because he was coming down in her direction. But after she recovered screaming, she found him lying on the other side, holding his ankle, and howling in pain. She felt guilty. If she didn't scream out of fear he probably would not have broken a bone. Worst comes to worst, they might've falter and fell together and she would've been the one underneath. So, Kaka found an excuse to come back early. She felt that he had suffered his injury in part because he was avoiding injuring her. She also worried that no one would take care of the lonesome figure in this dorm.

Are you sure that you didn't do it because you miss me? Lu Weijun closed the disposable container and poked a hole in the middle with a chopstick to save the environment. He felt that his broken ankle might be for the best, because if he had hit Kaka instead she would've fallen backwards with the back of her head hitting the ground. Let's see, as your savior, you should deliver my meal every day and keep me company. Then he laid down in bed. You should provide whatever services necessary. He couldn't help but snickered afterwards when he realized his last sentence might be misconstrued for another meaning.

Kaka raised her hand and pointed it at him across the table. She was smiling. She looked more natural now, and the mist in her eyes was gone. The distance they kept from each other for months was now a thing of the past.

When his ankle plaster was removed, Lu Weijun was already holding Kaka's hand.

The first time Xiqing saw Lu Weijun and Kaka holding hands was at the Manglu Bookstore. Lu Weijun was not at all prepared for the encounter and he seemed awkward. Kaka, on the other hand, reacted as if nothing was out of the ordinary. She said hello and asked how Xiqing was. They were students of different majors and had not run into each other ever since Xiqing moved out. Neither of them could say for sure who was trying to avoid whom. In the eyes of Kaka, Xiqing was always vacillating and at least part of her vacillation was done on purpose. She deliberately wished to be missed by Lu Weijun. She also purposefully embarrassed Lu Weijun in front of Kaka. In the past, she would use silence a hundred times to obscure her response to Lu Weijun, and now she would use silence to question Kaka's relationship with Lu Weijun. From the beginning to the end, Xiqing's response was confined to one word: fine and nothing else. When Kaka asked how she had been recently, she said she was fine. Kaka said she went to the Arts Museum with Lu Weijun the other day for an exhibition and spotted Xia Zheng's painting there as well. Xiqing's response was that it was fine. "We are going to eat now, so we'll leave you to continue with your browsing," Lu Weijun said. She stuck to the same response: fine.

Kaka let her displeasure show when they were outside. She felt that Lu Weijun rushed her out of the store out of guilty conscience. "A guilty conscience over what?" Lu Weijun said. "What is there to feel guilty about?" Kaka glared at him. You know better in your heart!

Similar dialogue was replayed seven years later outside the Extreme Gallery three years ago. When Lu Weijun spotted Xiqing standing before his own painting, he subconsciously took Kaka's hands beside him. At that very moment, Kaka felt her heart sink. She hadn't seen Xiqing for six or seven years.

After graduation, Kaka became a designer at a designing firm and Lu Weijun signed on as a contract artist by the S Gallery. He thought at first that the future looked bright for him, but after three years of good cooperation, their Jewish boss took nearly a thousand paintings by him and scores of other artists, and disappeared without a trace. Without being paid a cent, Lu Weijun found himself in dire financial straits. He and the others were thinking of suing their Jewish boss, but they were not famous artists to begin with and it would have to be a cross border lawsuit as well. They ended up only having their case registered at the police station, and every answer they got from the station afterwards was the same. The case is still being investigated. The investigation dragged on for years. Lu Weijun had a hot temper, and now that his paintings were gone and he had no means of support, he started throwing things at home and became verbally abusive, like a caged wounded animal. Kaka had been extremely understanding. She kept saying that things would get better, that everything would get better. Lu Weijun cried.

He only resumed painting a whole year later. Kaka also sensed clearly that he had become more reserved and quiet than before. He was no longer the trusting soul he once was and his temper became unpredictable. The good thing was everything indeed seemed to get better, and now Lu Weijun was able to participate in the joint exhibition at the Extreme Gallery.

Kaka remembered the painting. It was done on

a sunny day of his mercurial weather-like temper. The person he painted was Kaka in her school days, holding a book, leaning on a window, and staring into the distance. It was titled *Youthful Dream*. Kaka knew very well that aside from the looks, everything about the girl in the painting belonged to Xiqing. She was a vibrant and vivacious girl while in school and never looked so quiet and composed. She didn't have the expression of longing and expectation either. But Kaka kept this to herself, hoping that the sunny mood would last. Girls like Kaka had truly matured in their thinking after working for a few years. She felt that there were two stages in personal growth; during the first stage, one learned how to control one's body, and during the next stage, one learned to control oneself in that body. According to this way of thinking, Xiqing had long grown up, and so had Kaka. Lu Weijun, on the other hand, had never grown up. Or perhaps Lu Weijun was in the process of growing up, since he now knew to put the expression of Xiqing in the body of Kaka in his painting.

Lu Weijun just had a few words of formality with Xiqing. This time Kaka didn't seem to be that friendly either. She didn't even ask to exchange phone numbers with Xiqing. Kaka had been sizing up Xiqing during the two or three minute conversation.

She could sense very clearly that a certain aura that used to envelop Xiqing was all gone by now. She seemed to be sunnier than before. Seven years didn't seem to have left any marks on her looks. She showed some curiousness about Lu Weijun and asked what he was doing now, but Lu Weijun didn't feel like talking about what happened to him in the past several years. Dragging Kaka's hand, he said they needed to leave early for another show.

"As you can see, I don't have a guilty conscience," Lu Weijun said as if he was talking to himself when they were outside the gallery. Kaka glared at him as usual. You know better in your heart!

Not even Lu Weijun could have guessed that Xiqing had asked for his business card from Wang Yao. She claimed that she just wanted to talk about the old times with Kaka. That was how on a dark night he and Xiqing ended up sitting in a rundown cafe. Lu Weijun said he couldn't afford any high-class location but here.

Xiqing missed her period for more than a month now. Sitting outside the obstetric gynecology office and holding a patient information card with a fake name and fake age, she appeared restless. She didn't dare to tell Xia Zheng, neither did she want to, because Xia Zheng was preparing for the review necessary for his promotion from instructor to associate professor. The smell of disinfectant permeated the corridor. She went in to get a number and saw that it was a female doctor in her forties. There weren't many patients waiting, but she went to the lady's room anyway. She seemed to have a warm and sticky feeling in her lower abdomen and she just wanted to make sure.

At the entrance of the lady's room, she came face to face with Kaka who was just coming out. This was the first time she ran into Kaka since she moved out of the dormitory. Kaka seemed surprised to see her. Why are you at the hospital? Anything the matter? Kaka asked. I think I have the flu. Xiqing lied. Her sudden loss of nerves made her anxious to get into the lady's room as quickly as possible, so she didn't think to ask Kaka why she was here either. But then came the voice of Lu Weijun. Xiqing!

Kaka walked towards Lu Weijun and put her hands in his. He was able to get around by himself now, except that he still had an unusual limp. Xiqing turned and saw the gauze bandage on Lu Weijun's left ankle and his clutching tightly Kaka's hand. She was a little surprised but only inquired about his injury and recovery. In the lady's room, Xiqing saw a young girl with dyed blond hair who was no more than nineteen skillfully unpacking a pregnancy test kit. She glanced at the packaging that had the words "you be the first to know."

Li Jiajia! Is Li Jiajia here? The voice of the nurse rang in the corridor.

But Li Jiajia was heading for the drug store.

Lu Weijun had in fact spotted Xiqing a while ago. She was walking out of the Ob/Gyn office, paying no attention to her surroundings. He wanted to call her, but he thought of Kaka in the lady's room and hesitated. Before he knew it, Kaka and Xiqing ran into each other. His intuition and judgment were telling him that the reason for Xiqing's hospital visit was not as simple as a case of flu, but he didn't share his thoughts with Kaka. Rather he kept quiet on their way back. As they reached the entrance of the Tenth Dormitory, Kaka shook free her hand. I am going back to my dorm. She then went directly upstairs without turning once. All the anger she had suppressed inside her finally broke out in the open.

Lu Weijun understood why Kaka was outraged. He wished that she would come down and let him woo her, so he held his head high and cried out: 403, Bi Lu, 403, Bi Lu! But Kaka was conspicuously missing from all the heads that stuck out from the building.

Xiqing bought the kit from a drugstore and put it in her pocket. On her way, back her hand never left her pocket. Her thoughts were jumping rapidly from subject to subject, from the words Xia Zheng said to her last night to her possible pregnancy to the clasped hands of Lu Weijun and Kaka. In the past few months, spending time together with Xia Zheng and their living together all seemed very natural, as if this was the way it should be. She went to school during the day and so did he. They had lunch on their own in the school cafeteria and had supper together at the staff cafeteria. At home, she read books and he wrote books. Sometimes he would also stay up in his studio to finish his paintings in time for competition. Those were the years when Xia Zheng was making a name for himself. She didn't dare become his distractor.

But even when everything seemed so natural Xiqing still felt that there was something missing. Maybe it was because subconsciously she felt life was not challenging enough, because they had not been through many ups and downs. She liked Xia Zheng. She liked him very much, but what about Xia Zheng? It seemed that he was so sure of her and had everything under control before he would unknowingly say something, leaving her unsettled. Last night, Xia Zheng told Xiqing that if he didn't get the promotion this time he would resign and work at his friends' advertisement agency for a change. The words just flowed out gently, showing no signs of anxiety, as if he was not beating a retreat and was merely talking about what might happen to others. His treatment of Xiqing was also like that. He was nice, but not too nice. As they had this teacher-student relationship, they always walked one after another. If they ran into each other after class, they would each go their own way after a short exchange. Xiqing always felt a sense of loss when she saw other girls smiling sweetly on the shoulders of their boyfriends. When she was not in love she was alone, now that she was in love she was even more alone sometimes. She was surprised to see Lu Weijun and Kaka today, but after careful consideration, she knew that it was an understandable development.

As she approached the staff dormitory, Xiqing spotted Lu Weijun, still holding an aluminum alloy cane, sitting on a stone bench, newly grown stubbles now covered his shaved head. He stood up and walked towards her slowly. "What was the result?" He asked without any formality. Xiqing didn't respond. She just looked at him. She didn't even know the results herself.

They sat down on the long bench. Xiqing asked him about his ankle injury, talked about her going back to her hometown for the funeral of her sister, and then she inquired about the relationship between Lu Weijun and Kaka. All seemed quiet, as if two old friends who hadn't seen each other for some time were catching up. But for whatever reason, sitting next to Lu Weijun today, Xiqing felt that she could sense his body temperature, which made her anxious.

Even towards the end Xiqing never admitted to her possible pregnancy. She asked Lu Weijun if the sketches he did about her were done before ever setting eyes on her. Lu Weijun nodded emphatically.

By the time Xia Zheng came home, Xiqing had seen the two dark red lines on the test strip. She threw the strip in the garbage, took the garbage out, and sat on the sofa lost in thought. The strange thing was that she was not at all flustered or confused, as if everything was normal and natural as it could be. She didn't think carefully of what to do next, but the image of Zhuqing that summer came up. She also thought of her nephew Wu Zuo and felt sad, as if the same thing was going to play out on her.

Xia Zheng took off his shoes, sat down on the sofa, reached out an arm to hold her close, and asked about her day. Did you go to the auditorium for the seminar on going directly to graduate school? Xiqing nodded her head numbly and then shook it.

Kaka just woke up from her dream when the plane landed at the capital airport. She felt numbness in her right arm, as if tens of thousands of needles were prickling her. She turned around and found her right hand in the palm of Dino Fabou, who was looking at the snow outside the airplane window coming down in distinct flakes. Through Wang Yao's connection, Kaka had had several art critics ready in Beijing to "drum up" the name of Xia Zheng. On matters like this Dino Fabou liked to stay behind the scene. He will only meet with Lang Qiaozhi across the hall at the last auction in Hanhai.

As they disembarked, Kaka phoned Xia Zheng. She wanted to know if he had arrived in Beijing. We are in a cab on our way to the hotel but are stuck now near the Sanyuan Bridge, Xia Zheng replied. Checking the scene along the way, Kaka saw that Beijing seemed cleaner than a year ago. Most of the fenced-in construction sites in preparation for the Olympics were about to finish their work, ready for the new look. When their car went past the Workers' Stadium she thought of Lu Weijun. Seven or eight years ago when they were still students they had visited Beijing for art exhibitions and concerts. Without that many construction sites as they did now, the city then was still covered in grey, and yellow sands always found their way in raindrops. She wanted to try calling Lu Weijun again, but Dino Fabou was right beside her.

Xiqing and Wu Zuo once again sat across a long table facing each other. Only this time they were at the detention center. Wu Zuo looked a little haggard with a sallow face and rumpled hair. His gold-rimmed glasses were bent out of shape. He said he crushed them this morning when he turned to get up. He kept on sniffling and his body shuddered every time he sniffled. His words were not as steady and crisp as they once were. Lu Weijun was still in a coma in the hospital. Although the doctors claimed that his life was no longer in danger they left the exact time he could come out of coma to God. Hence Wu Zuo's stay at the detention center was also up to God.

In the hospital, the family members of Lu Weijun gave Xiqing a really hard time. They cried and asked for compensation far above the medical costs. Of course the figure was based on the understanding that Lu Weijun would wake up one day, and if he didn't wake up in three months, everything would be up for renegotiation! The one who did the crying and howling was Lu Weijun's aunt, but Xiqing knew very well that the one who was determined to make things hard for her was Lu Weijun's cousin. When she entered the ICU with the tonics she bought, she felt unsettled and expected as much.

Are you mad at me? Wu Zuo sniffled.

Xiqing stared at him. I just feel sorry for you.

Lately I've been dreaming about my mom, the mom who always looked the way she was in the picture on display in your bedroom. But you know that later on, later on she became a changed person. Her face went dark and she was always in fear. Wu Zuo rubbed the corner of his eyes with his hand. The gold-rimmed glasses were truly bent out of shape.

My sister wouldn't like to see you sitting here. Xiqing was angry inside. She also felt guilty. The reason why Wu Zuo was sitting here definitely had something to do with her. Still, she couldn't understand why Wu Zuo became so emotional and violent which was so out of his character. She still remembered the smile she discerned on Wu Zuo's face when the bloody-headed Lu Weijun crumbled at the studio door. The muscle spasm that appeared with the smile really gave Xiqing chills. After about ten seconds she gave a shriek, letting out all the dread and panic inside her. It was then that

Wu Zuo dropped paralyzed into a dining chair, his eyes two empty dry wells.

The other person, how is he doing? Wu Zuo asked. He held his head so low that he dared not look at Xiqing in the eye.

He hasn't come to yet. There is no need for you to worry. The doctors said that he will wake up in a few days. Xiqing tried to comfort him.

He'd better never wake up. Wu Zuo murmured to himself in a low voice.

Xia Zheng and Wang Yao were on each side of the back seat of a taxi. Since both had things on their mind they didn't talk much. Xia Zheng was still trying to figure out how Lu Weijun was attacked at his place, whereas Wang Yao was thinking of the phone call yesterday afternoon from Lang Qiaozhi's assistant. The taxi got stuck at SanYuan Bridge right after getting off the airport overpass, but they only noticed that when Kaka called Xia Zheng, who then looked outside.

Xiqing didn't tell Xia Zheng about Wu Zuo's attack of Lu Weijun immediately after his return from the U.S. He learned it from their neighbors. The broken lock to his studio also attested to what happened. There were signs of violent strikes on the groove. That night, Xia Zheng made love to Xiqing with reckless abandon. He told himself to lay all suspicion and anger aside absolutely and completely, and concentrated on kissing, caressing, and making his moves, but this was also the first time that he felt that he was not exactly in full command of his body. In the dim light the white flesh of Xiqing seemed so young to Xia Zheng, while he himself was in decline.

Are they here too? Wang Yao turned and asked. Do you have tomorrow afternoon's speech prepared?

Xia Zheng nodded. When it comes to giving speeches, he hasn't had any practice since he left school. But just like any other skill that you once were good at, after a hiatus of eight or nine years you might become a bit rusty but you could surely handle it with relative ease. The title to Xia Zheng's speech was *The Return to Position of the Chinese Contemporary Art*, just the opposite of the topic of his New York seminar ten years ago. In the last decade, as a painter and an artist whose market importance had been constantly on the rise, he had experienced first hand the ups and downs and vicissitudes of the market, and through it all he must have grasped also the laws governing the market as well.

The taxi inched forward in the slow-moving traffic.

As it was about to reach the Agricultural Exhibition Hall a call came in from Xiqing. When he took his phone out of his pocket he had the premonition that it was a call from Xiqing. He had had such strong premonitions before. They have lived together for ten years. There was unexplained sixth sense phenomenon between the two that went very deep. This time, somehow, the call from Xiqing caused resentment and suspicion on his part. Xiqing was merely asking about his arrival in Beijing, the weather, his health, and the ensuing arrangement, but they sounded like formalities to him. Xia Zhent sensed for the first time that as a man his sensitive feelings were hurt. He wanted very much to find out what exactly was going on, but he didn't. It is not that he didn't know how to start he just didn't know how it would end. He was afraid that once he asked, the end would be hard for both of them.

As far as Xia Zheng could recall, Xiqing rarely took the initiative and called when he went to other places for exhibitions or meetings. This was at least his general impression. In fact, he never made note of such details and never remembered who called whom. Usually, he only took out his cellphone and called Xiqing when he suddenly remembered her existence. Even then, the conversation was mostly short and limited to matters of routine. Where are you? Have you had something? I will be back the day after tomorrow, or something like that. Sometimes he would think of asking about her health and how come she sounded so exhausted only after he hung up the phone and suddenly realized that her voice sounded tired. But he would always get distracted right afterwards by Wang Yao's request to attend to something else or meet with other collectors. Then all his concern for Xiqing would unwittingly dissipate like vapor.

After hanging up, Xia Zheng felt bitter. He used the thumb and index finger of his right hand to rub the point between his eyes, and heaved a slight sigh. He felt something was pressing hard against his chest and he was tired.

After her phone call to Xia Zheng, Xiqing walked towards Lu Weijun's place. She had an appointment with someone, someone she hadn't seen for almost twenty years. She knew that he still remembered her, just as she recognized him right away at the hospital.

Xu Xiqing. He was waiting for her on the stone bench by the flowerbed, with one hand holding the leash for Luka and another holding the newspaper.

Shan Linjian. Xiqing said.

Oh? You still remember my name? He stood up, raising his eyebrows. He had his trademarked black-rimmed glasses over the nose bridge and he had a self-righteous looking face. It was this face that caused loathing by most of his classmates more than ten years ago. At the time, Xiqing didn't have any strong feeling towards anyone, but she was scared to read the classical poem *The Reeds and Rushes*. It was a period of growing up most susceptible to forming cliques at the exclusion of others, and she was so afraid that she would be isolated by the rest of the class.

The talks were centered on whether they would file a complaint against Wu Zuo. The way Shan Linjian moved his lips and pushed his eyeglasses was the same way as in his high school days. So, could you tell me why Lu Weijun was injured at your place? What exactly is your relationship with him?

Xiqing stuck to her version, one she had worked out with Wu Zuo. She said that Lu Weijun was there to see Xia Zheng. He was hoping to participate in young artist joint exhibitions. The innocent quarrel he started with Wu Zuo later degenerated into a physical fight. Even Xiqing found the story not totally believable. There were simply too many holes to it. Although the police didn't challenge the truthfulness of the story at the station, when it was retold to Shan

Linjian she felt that every word of hers was being reviewed and examined with contempt.

To Xiqing's surprise, Shan Linjian broke into a smile after listening to her story. Without saying a word and still wearing a smile, he scooped Luka into his arms and walked towards Lu Weijun's place. After taking a few more steps, he burst out with a loud and boisterous laugh. After another ten steps or so, he suddenly turned around and said very slowly and emphatically: Xu—Xi—Qing—YOU—ARE—A—HYPOCRITE, just like you were in high school!

Staring at the back of Shan Linjian, Xiqing was on the verge of crying. She never felt so bad in her life. She was deeply ashamed of herself and the embarrassment was all too real. Ten years ago, Kaka also accused her of being hypocritical and insincere, saying that she would love to be loved by all the men in this world! Xiqing denied it at the time. She also denied it emphatically in her heart. But today she found she was unable to defend herself, as if the confidence she once had was so crushed and crumbled into a corner, withering, and she finally had to admit to her hypocrisy.

But hypocrisy is a coat that many people have worn for some time. Only they themselves are not aware of them ever putting it on.

Arriving home, Xiqing pushed open the door to the studio. The damaged lock fell to the ground, making a particularly unpleasant sound when hitting the cement. All Xia Zheng's paintings sold at auctions were here. Some of them had been in the private storage room of Wang Yao, but were moved here as water seeped into the storage room during the monsoon season. This was a secret shared only by Xia Zheng and Wang Yao and no one else. The rising values at auctions were meant to have all of hem resold at a future date. In the last few years, because of the sheer number of Xia Zheng's works in his collection, Wang Yao devoted almost all his energy to raise the value of Xia Zheng's painting. He knew very well that once they were in Dino Fabou's hands, he would have a constant flow of money coming in. Once he had the financial base, he can devote his efforts on another artist and reap huge profits by having his investment grow in this market in an even shorter time cycle.

Xiqing flipped through the paintings on wooden frames and was lost in her thoughts. Indeed, Xia Zheng's skills had matured over the years, but his later works also showed an increasing lack of spirituality, something that would only appear with ardor and life. Xiqing didn't know if all these paintings looked so dull to her was because ardor was amiss in her life. She sighed, closed her eyes and felt that everything was so quiet all around her, a quiet before the chaos. She knew that the chaos was coming. Things would be different after Xia Zheng's Beijing trip. The chaos that was latent now would erupt from everywhere. They would become rich.

At this moment, Xiqing felt that if time could go backwards, she would rather that Xia Zheng was still teaching in school, and was her "husband." He would paint occasionally and his paintings would carry fully his zeal for life, his happiness or sadness. She thought of the child who was aborted before taking shape and became immersed in immense sorrow and grief.

9

The meeting of Dino Fabou and Lang Qiaozhi didn't take place at any auction houses, but instead through their respective assistants they arranged to have dinner. They had a tacit understanding that overly secretive and quiet environment was not to their liking. They would like to find a place surrounded by people, with bodies moving about from time to time, hence their selection of a restaurant buffet. For three whole hours, neither Dino Fabou nor Lang Qiaozhi made reference to anything related to auctions. They only talked about arts, literature, interspersed with the occasional chatter about interesting tourism spots in China, as if they were old friends. Listening to their conversation while eating, Kaka was thinking more of the way they carried it out. They both knew why they were there but no one would approach the subject. This showed how skillful Dino Fabou and Lang Qiaozhi were.

Kaka learned from Xia Zheng the circumstances that led to Lu Weijun's injury and hospitalization. In her mind, she knew exactly what had happened. This was also the first time after leaving China that she thought of the possible dubious, sexual relationship or inexplicable obsession between Lu Weijun and Xiqing. But right now, she was no longer Lu Weijun's girlfriend, neither was she Xiqing's good friend. She was merely an observer, or more recently, a woman who had made love several times with Lu Weijun on Skype. She had told herself a thousand times that she should not feel angry or hurt, because what had happened had nothing to do with her.

But after numberous self-comforting efforts, Kaka, without the knowledge of Dino Fabou, still booked a round-trip ticket to Shanghai from Beijing. She was thinking that she could ask for a day off, taking an early flight in the morning and coming back in the afternoon. She told herself that she was making the trip for baby Luka.

The meeting between Wang Yao and Lang Qiaozhi took place in secrecy. Lang Qiaozhi asked his assistant to arrange the meeting in a private room at a western restaurant. What they talked about was quite simple and direct. Lang Qiaozhi hoped that Wang Yao would cede to him all of Xia Zheng's pieces that he had in his possession after the auction, and that he was willing to pay a price ten percent higher than Dino Fabou's offer. His purpose was simple; it was necessary to make an initial show of strength in their first battle. Wang Yao didn't agree right away; he said he still needed some time to think it over. But on his way back to the hotel, he received a call from Lang Qiaozhi's assistant that they would like to increase their offer by another two percentage points. That was their highest limit.

What do they say? Kaka was already on the sofa when he returned to his room.

Their final offer was twelve percent higher than Dino Fabou's. Wang Yao loosened his tie and plumped down right next to Kaka in a sweeping gesture, hoping to embrace her, but Kaka adroitly evaded his advance.

Don't forget that you promised Dino Fabou, who is definitely not to be trifled with. Kaka got two cans of beverage from the refrigerator and threw one to Wang Yao.

That is why I let you in on this information. What do you take me for, a moron? Someone who only look at the money and nothing else?

No, you are not a moron, but you do look only at the money. You gave me this piece of information for the sole purpose of having me pass it on to Dino Fabou so that you can get an even better price from him.

Kaka's words were like a blade pointing directly at Wang Yao. He looked at Kaka with nodded approval.

You have come a long way from where you were several years ago. You haven't been going around with Dino Fabou for nothing. But rest assured that once the deal concerning Xia Zheng goes through I will certainly do my best to make your Lu Weijun a star. With the experience we've accumulated, his value would climb even faster than Xia Zheng's. What's more, he's still young and has a great future ahead of him.

This is what you promised me four years ago, but Lu Weijun's paintings are still languishing in galleries.

Kaka still felt upset when talking about Lu Weijun, but she kept it all inside her. The thought of his embarrassing situation today only aroused her sorrow.

Four years ago what prompted Kaka to split with Lu Weijun and go with Dino Fabou, aside from the knowledge that Lu Weijun and Xiqing were seeing each other in secret, was mostly because she was hoping that through her connections with Dino Fabou and Wang Yao, she could be of some help to Lu Weijun someday and get him out of his predicament. She also knew well that her departure might speed up what was going on between Lu Weijun and Xiqing, but her heart was already broken and she was still in love with Lu Weijun. The only choice she had then was leaving. She didn't tell Lu Weijun the purpose of her study in the United States, and he had always assumed that the reappearance of Xiqing was what caused his breaking up with Kaka.

After getting the information relayed by Kaka, Dino Fabou decided to have a talk with Wang Yao alone.

When Kaka hugged Luka in her arms, he responded by licking her hands like an old friend. His tongue was moist and warm; one lick had reduced Kaka to tears. When she saw the familiar setting inside her place, the curtains she herself selected and the sparrows on the terrace she hadn't seen for so long, old memories just hit her like waves. How are you? She put Luka down on the floor. Luka wagged his tail and barked at her, as if he could understand what she was saying. She noted the pile of unpaid bills in the key dish at the entryway. Lu Weijun was still so forgetful. To Kaka, that was a day that seemed very short, and also very long.

Kaka went to see Lu Weijun at the hospital. He was deep in his sleep. Because they often saw each other on the Internet, he wasn't an unfamiliar sight to her. But when she touched his face with her hand, something seemed to have gripped her heart, and the pain reached all the way to her fingertips, rendering them limp and numb. She was uncharacteristically hesitant. Patient history was clipped on a board by the side of the bed. Kaka went through the daily report carefully. Although he hadn't woken up, there was every indication that he was getting better. The CTs were showing that the blood clot was actually getting smaller. After reading the patient history, she walked towards Lu Weijun and put the pile of paid bills underneath his pillow, bent down, and kissed him. The smooth breathing sound coming from Lu Weijun fluttered through Kaka's cheeks. At that moment, the thought of not returning to Beijing crossed her mind.

Kaka? Xiqing stopped in her steps, feeling unsure herself. She in fact had recognized Kaka through the glass door.

Kaka turned her head, recognizing Xiqing's voice. Let's talk outside.

Xiqing followed Kaka to a grapevine trellis downstairs outside the hospital with the vicious noonday sun dappling down through the leaves. Xiqing lowered her head like a student who did wrong and was waiting for the teacher's ruling. Kaka leaned against a concrete column and examined her in an unfriendly manner.

What happened to Lu Weijun? Kaka asked.

Xiqing raised her head, met her eyes, and lowered her head immediately again. She was about to lie but stopped when she realized that her elaborate lies sounded so lame.

Xiqing paused before finally managing to tell Kaka what really happened that day. She felt so relieved afterwards, but dared not to think what would come next. Four years ago when Kaka found her at Lu Weijun's place, she knew that she would lose Kaka forever.

You are so disgusting. Kaka said. She appeared calm but her eyes were full of anger. If you are in love with Xia Xheng, stay with Xia Zheng. If you are in love with Lu Weijun, stay with Lu Weijun. Why do you always have to have both of them in your life? Will you only be satisfied when both have literally fallen head over heels for you?

Xiqing didn't respond, looking extremely embarrassed.

Do you think remaining silent will get you off the hook? Indeed, that was your favorite tactic during school days, but I am telling you now that as far as I, Bi Lu, is concerned, this tactic is useless! Kaka stared at her. The flame of her inexplicable anger at the bottom of her heart simply grew more violent. She knew that she had no right to get angry or pour out her anger at Xiqing. After all, who was she? Who was Lu Weijun to her? And what right did she have to fault others? Xiqing stopped being her best friend four years ago, so she had lost the right to lose her temper before a close friend too.

Kaka turned and left, refusing to face Xiqing's provocative silence any longer. The seemingly moving silence would probably make her wonder if she had gone too far, and she didn't want the burden of this guilt, nor did she wish to expose her own weakness in the end.

Kaka. Xiqing called after her. But she didn't

stop walking. Whatever happens will happen. The friendship formed when they were young had long gone sour. She didn't need it any more.

Lu Weijun woke up. The first person he saw when he opened his eyes was Kaka, but in an instant Kaka just disappeared. He felt that he had been in a long dream but he couldn't recall anything about the dream. He tried hard to remember what happened before he lost consciousness. He was at Xiqing's place. He went there fuming with a bottle of 94 Great Wall. The instant he broke opened Xia Zheng's studio he saw the paintings of Xia Zheng. Those that caught his attention were the ones with high prices fetched at auctions. Everything became clear to him now.

Lu Weijun shook himself loose in the bed. Looking at the ceiling that was poorly painted, he tried moving the fingers on his right hand and felt the prickling pain of the IV needle. Then he tried to move his left hand, his left foot, and his right foot. He could still feel them and was thus relieved. But after lying there for too long, he still didn't have the energy to sit up or to make any vigorous movement. He could only guess the number of days he had been in the hospital. Not long afterwards Xiqing pushed open the door and entered. Lu Weijun immediately closed his eyes.

His grievances and anger towards Xiqing were long forgotten after his many days of deep sleep. He merely wanted to play a trick on her.

Xiqing had been crying all the way up from downstairs. She felt that she had been frozen the minute she saw Kaka in the hospital room and never recovered, which was why she was unable to respond to Kaka's scolding. She only recovered as if waking up suddenly from a dream, when Kaka turned her back on her. She knew that she owed Kaka three words: I am sorry. But those words never came out of her mouth. She was crying now because she realized that even if she had said those words they would not have made any difference. She had lost Kaka a long time ago.

The hospital room had the smell of old disinfectant that refused to go away even with fresh air circulating for a month. Xiqing sat by Lu Weijun's bedside. His hair was again shaved clean because the doctors wanted to have him ready for brain surgery to clear his blood clot, so he now looked more like his old self in his college days. In the last ten years, Lu Weijun didn't seem to have aged. He was the least changed out of all of them. He still worked hard, was undisciplined, willful, and headstrong as ever.

Xiqing reached out her hand to touch Lu Weijun's face, but withdrew it midway. She cried at his bedside, heartbroken. So many people went through her mind. Kaka, Lu Weijun, Xia Zheng, Wu Zuo, her sister, and even Shan Linjian. She was overwhelmed with feelings. She felt Shan Linjian was right when he called her a hypocrite.

Lu Weijun wanted to open his eyes to surprise Xiqing, but he heard crying and could sense also that she was trembling. He remembered the Xiqing from ten years ago. He remembered Kaka. He remembered Xia Zheng. He remembered the tangles they had gotten into in the past ten years and his heart sank. His body became stiff. He could only let Xiqing cry, while he himself struggled with mixed emotions.

Before leaving Shanghai, Shan Linjian returned a picture to Xiqing. It was a picture he took without her knowing, a picture his cousin once stole a look at because of his own carelessness. Even Lu Weijun himself didn't remember this, but that glimpse had resulted in the appearance of Xiqing in his dreams.

10

Xia Zheng was feeling tired after participating in yet another seminar. He was waiting for a taxi on a broad street under the burning Beijin sun, while Wang Yao stood next to him yammering about his next scheduled event. He could sense his increasingly palpitating heartbeats and shortness of breath. In the past few days, he had been running from the east side to the west side, from the Military Museum to the International Trade Building. He made appearances at seminars and press conferences, and he gave many speeches as well. He hardly had any time to rest and he couldn't sleep well at night either. He couldn't get his mind off the incident concerning Lu Weijun. He felt that he was losing his physical strength and was about to be suffocated.

Another symposium is set for you at the Xidan Library Building in a little while. Do you have your material ready? Wang Yao asked. Although he also felt the terrible heat and the exhaustion, he was excited nevertheless, seeing that his hard work over the last few years was finally about to come to fruition. Truth be told, it was finally about to turn to cash. He floored the gas paddle in his all-encompassing arrangements for Xia Zheng, and hoped for the best results at the auctions that were to be held in a few days. By then, the value of Xia Zheng's paintings would climb to a new high. Instead of making the small steps as they have been doing in the past few years, this time it would shoot up in leaps! Yes, leaps! Every time Wang Yao thought of the word "leaps," he couldn't help but smile like a flower from inside out. Little did he know that an accident would happen at a time when he was the most confident.

As Xia Zheng sat down by the lectern and reached to move the microphone in front of him, the world before him suddenly went dark. His body slumped, but his hand was still in a raised position out of habit. And that was how those in the audience saw Xia Zheng's hand slowly sank below the lectern, making a loud noise. No one knew what had gone wrong seemingly for a long while.

Xia Zheng felt that he was suffocating. He tried to unbutton his shirt with his hand, but soon the boiling cooled down and he sensed an eerie kind of calm. All his worry, anxiety, and agitation were gone in an instant. He fell heavily to the ground, but he rose up again as he became weightless. It was a lightening-speed relief. He no longer cared about the prices on the auction market, nor did he entertain any hopes for a future with Xiqing. He only felt that he was tired, very tired, and he didn't see any happiness in his future.

That was how Xia Zheng's life ended so abruptly at the symposium. The doctor later confirmed that he died of a heart attack.

Xia Zheng's death became the headline news of the arts section of important newspapers at several major cities. As a young artist who had won critical reviews in the art world, who had seen his work commanding ever increasing prices, his untimely death undoubtedly left many collectors deploring his departure, for he hadn't had the time to establish himself in the art world and neither would there be any new paintings from him. Thus, the value of his paintings started to slip at a speed unexpected by Wang Yao. He now regretted that he didn't sign a contract with Dino Fabou the last time they met alone. At that time it was greed that had held him back. He was hoping to get an even better offer through his leverage of Lang Qiaozhi. He never expected that he would be losing both the artist and his fortune.

Lu Weijun learned about Xia Zheng's sudden death from the newspaper. That was the day he was about to leave the hospital. He had promised Xiqing that he would not file a complaint against Wu Zuo. He also found a pile of paid bills underneath his pillow. He was stunned by the news and didn't recover for a long while. This was the first time in his almost thirty years of life that he had a first-hand experience of what "life is unpredictable" meant. He suddenly realized that no one would know if he or she would still be alive tomorrow. So, Lu Weijun decided to look for Kaka in Beijing. He wanted to bring Kaka back so that they, along with Luka, could start a life together.

Xiqing didn't cry at Xia Zheng's funeral. She couldn't bring herself to cry before an urn. Wang Yao on the other hand was crying his heart out. No one could tell how much of his crying was for the memory of Xia Zheng, and how much was from bitterness and regret. Lu Weijun was present also. He bowed deeply and murmured several times that he was sorry. He held a secret, a secret only he himself knew. Ten years ago, it was he who wrote the letter to the department, accusing Xia Zheng of getting a student pregnant, thus forcing him to hand in his resignation and leave the school. If not for the letter things might turn out differently. But there is no if in the world, is there? Lu Weijun took a deep breath. If there is, he would rather that he never had those fancy youthful dreams, never loved Xiqing who looked exactly like the girl in his dreams, and never lost his mind to jealousy and hurt. He knew very well that Xia Zheng's calm resignation of his post was meant to clear the way for Xiqing to enter graduate school without trouble. He didn't want her to be negatively affected by unnecessary complications. This had made Lu Weijun realize that he had lost. He lost because he failed to understand what love was.

Whatever happened then, Xia Zheng took it all upon himself without protest. He never shared it with Xiqing. He was always the responsible one, including his responsibility to love, which weighed him down, until his death.

After auction Dino Fabou went back to New York alone. He left a check with Kaka, telling her that she earned it. He also gave her a solid embrace and kiss. But Kaka stuffed the check in a garbage can as soon as she stepped outside the airport. She was grateful to Dino Fabou for all he taught her in the last few years, but she was not willing to link her body with money. Now, she could stand alone as an art broker. She would like to help out Lu Weijun by relying on her own strength.

Wang Yao came to see Xiqing several times. He wanted to get back the paintings that were stored at Xia Zheng's place, but Xiqing suddenly disappeared. The school was telling him that Xiqing left as soon as Wu Zuo's judgment came down: two years of reeduacation through labor for causing accidental injury to others. Much, much later, someone spotted a shoot of blue smoke up the hills of Panyu, together with the sea of red at the foot of the hill it looked very much like an oil painting in despair.

Xiqing burned all Xia Zheng's paintings, the paintings that drove them further and further apart in those years, until they were never to meet again. Choking on her own tears, she watched the burning, still thinking "what ifs."

A Trilogy

The Ring

This is this year's last fly-back.

Walking out of the airport, Lin Zhuo telephoned Xu Wu who told her that the tickets back to Enze Township were already bought. As the New Year was fast approaching, there were long lines at the taxi stand. Lin Zhuo had no choice but to drag her luggage for the airport bus. Weighed down by the things that were on her mind, she struggled for quite some time with the luggage in tow. She never paid so much attention to her pace of homecoming. Slow down a bit, even slower, the slower the better. It would be best if the plane had arrived late, or if the bus had broken down.

As the bus left Pudong and went westward, scenery along the highway showed a gradual increase of human life. She noticed houses, water, animals, and small tractors, followed by hypermarkets, home furnishing centers, and residential areas until the bus passed the Lupu Bridge. Aside from that phone call, she hadn't sent any text messages to Xu Wu, as if this had already become part of her habit. She could still remember the old days when they first fell in love and when they were newlyweds. Every time she flew back, Xu Wu would always meet her at the airport, and if he was detained by work and couldn't meet her up in person, they would send numerous text messages to each other once her plane hit the ground until she arrived home. Once home, she would invariably find white roses on the dining table that Xu Wu had bought the night before, and the roses after a wait overnight would be madly in bloom. Lin Zhuo loved white roses very much, and *White Rose* was her favorite novel during her school days. White roses, according to the book, are preferred by people who have a quiet demeanor and are independent and strong. Lin Zhuo actually was not that strong or independent, but she might be considered a quiet type. But after seven years of work, she figured she had already been kneaded into a white rose by time and life experience, even if there would no longer be any blossoming roses greeting her return nowadays.

Xu Wu was already there when she arrived home. To her surprise, he had prepared a full course dinner, and a bunch of white roses were present on one side of the table. At the sight of Lin Zhuo, he greeted her with opened arms. This would have been their first hug after more than six months of cold war. But Lin Zhuo found this intimacy somewhat awkward now. She avoided his arms by bending down to untie her shoes. Xu Wu stood at the entrance feeling rebuffed, but after a short pause, he reached to take care of her luggage in a gesture to warm up the atmosphere.

I prepared some dishes, Xu Wu said. We haven't dined together at home for quite some time.

Oh. Lin Zhuo took off her scarf and walked towards the kitchen. She needed to wash her hands and adjust her mental state. The kitchen looked as new as the year they first got married. It had not accumulated grime or showed any signs of age. Because Lin Zhuo was not good at cooking, nor did she care much about cooking, they often ate out, sometimes just the two of them, sometimes each with their own friends. Occasionally, Xu Wu would cook at home. But every time he cooked, it was always followed by a deeply romantic night of lovemaking. Xu Wu had a healthy sexual drive, and so did Lin Zhuo. In the first three years of their marriage, she got pregnant twice, but she lost both babies in the first two months of pregnancy. At first, she didn't pay much attention to it, because as a consultant, she needed to fly to different places year round. She thought the exhaustive work had caused her miscarriages. But in the fourth year when she quit her job and rested at home during her third pregnancy, yet she once again lost the baby a few days short of two months, both Lin Zhuo and Xu Wu took notice. They went to many hospitals to seek help and were met with the same conclusion: habitual abortion. Doctors recommended that in view of her already delicate physical condition she should take precaution in avoiding pregnancy, or she might run the life-threatening risk of another miscarriage. Upon returning home from the hospital, Lin Zhuo and Xu Wu both passed a sleepless night.

The tap water somehow chilled her to the bone. Lin Zho put some soap on and rubbed her hands again and again. The delicate gold ring on her left ring finger was a gift from the father of Xu Wu before they got married. It was said that the gold ring was passed on from his mother, a real piece of heirloom. So, after coming back to Shanghai, they made a special trip to a jewelry store and had a replica made for Xu Wu for his wedding ring. Many of her colleagues liked her ring. There were some inscriptions carved on the ring. Some guessed that it was in Sanskrit; some thought they were ancient phonetics. There were even people who, after taking a look at it, decided that they were a string of nectars (amrita).

Lin Zhuo had looked at the ring for 5 years. She also felt that the carvings of magic symbols looked like a string of nectars.

All of a sudden, Xu Wu wrapped her into his arms from behind, holding her by her waist. Let's eat now, he lowered his head and said. Lin Zhuo was caught by surprise. She tried to get out of his grip by raising her shoulders but she hit his chin instead. He immediately saw stars. What are you doing? Xu Wu was irked. Lin Zhuo got sore too, and they again stopped talking to each other.

At night, Xu Wu tried to touch Lin Zhuo with his legs under his comforter. She pretended to be asleep and stayed motionless. She was staring at the windows as Xu Wu heaved a heavy sigh. They started using separate comforters more than six months ago because she didn't want Xu Wu to touch her. She was afraid of becoming pregnant. After her fourth miscarriage, she became so weak during her mini-confinement that she could hardly muster the energy to speak. She then made up her mind that she wouldn't try to have kids anymore. But Xu Wu was the sole male offspring in his family for three generations. The decision of having no children is not a viable choice, even having a girl child as the first born would not stop the grandparents from asking their daughter-in-law to give another try. This had become a bone of contention between the two numerous times. He would argue for another try and she would give him a hard and icy look. You want to sacrifice my life for your family's sake?

In order to reduce the possibilities of the two of them sleeping together, Lin Zhuo grabbed every opportunity to be on assignment that year. As a consultant, field missions could last from a week to a couple of months. Although the company would agree to pay for the perks of weekly fly-backs, she tried not to take advantage of it as much as possible. Home was no longer attractive to her. Xu Wu was rarely mentioned in her conversations with others. Sometimes, when she saw her colleagues were happily met at the airport by their husbands, or shared long and intimate talks with someone over the phone in hotel rooms, she would feel lost. She would also like them to be deeply in love as they were before, but nowadays they fought every time they were on the phone. Sweet and tender words from Xu Wu would inexplicably make her tense up. She felt that her husband was trying to coax her home so that they could sleep together and she could get pregnant. She was afraid, so afraid that her fear had turned into anger that needed to be let out. After a while, Xu Wu seeing her behavior as totally irrational would give up any attempt to sweet-talk her any longer.

As it was customary, this year they would spend the New Year at Xu Wu's hometown Enze. Lin Zhuo knew that she could no longer hide the truth and lie to her father-in-law. She was ready to tell him that she couldn't bear children, not that she would rather die than have children, but that she could die for having children. She understood why Xu Wu did the cooking himself tonight. It was meant to be his final attempt in finding out her true state of mind before going home. They had not made love for quite some time, even the few times they did he was asked by Lin Zhuo to use a condom throughout, and she would immediately take a long shower afterwards. Xu Wu was obviously bothered by this. He felt that as far as their sex life was concerned all his efforts were in vain, because his partner simply didn't know how to enjoy it.

Love is an enjoyment, and so is physical intimacy. A distracted partner could only destroy the mood. Gradually, Xu Wu lost his sexual desire and their love was on the brink. As Lin Zhuo became distracted during sex, he had also slipped somewhat from the moral high ground by having a new love interest, a young and vivacious intern at his company. But age had suppressed his youthful impulses, and the thirty-three-year-old Xu Wu kept his bodily desire in check.

Even if he did crave for a reckless and abandoned lovemaking, he just couldn't let go of the seven years of emotional entanglement with Lin Zhuo. He knew that there were things once done that would be very hard to undo. The girl was very nice to him and he was very nice to her. She bought breakfast for him everyday, and he gave her daily rides back to school after work. Sometimes, Xu Wu rather enjoyed such lucid and platonic affection. It brought warmth to him in the winter, much like the cup of heartwarming tea that the elders at Enze shared in the afternoon. He never said a word, but the girl could no longer keep her silence. One day, she confessed to him in tears that she liked him. After returning home, Xu Wu just couldn't go to sleep. Every time he closed his eyes he would see those red and swollen teary eyes.

That night in his dream Xu Wu saw his mother. She was in her thirties, looked matronly and kind. She was sitting under the light of a desk lamp mending a pair of socks for his father. His father was the furnace tenderer at the county crematory. Legend has it that people doing that kind of work have to guard themselves well with thick and full clothing with no holes anywhere, lest the bad spirit might sneak in. Hence, his mother would carefully check his father's clothing everyday, making sure that the loose threads and holes were well taken care of. A while later, his father walked behind his mother, tapped her shoulders a few times and she would follow him shyly into another room. Xu Wu was six at the time. Not knowing what was going on, he peeked from underneath the door curtain. The naked body of her mother was very white, and her lying on top of his father looked like a piece of white jade in mud. He didn't know what they were doing at the time and only realized when he himself became an adult that he was actually witnessing the lovemaking of his parents. Later his mother died of hemorrhagic miscarriage. His father was the one who brought up Xu Wu single-handedly from age ten. He thus became a very obedient son to his father and never went against his will.

The death of Xu Wu's mother also weighed heavily on Lin Zhuo's mind. She felt that it should serve as a warning to herself.

The next morning when Lin Zhuo woke up, she noticed that Xu Wu was already awake staring at the ceiling. After a long while, he finally said something: Let's get a divorce. When I get back home tomorrow I will ask my father for the residence booklet.

Uh huh. Lin Zhuo was taken aback, but she suppressed her emotions. She turned to lie on her side and tried to stay in bed a little longer. Xu Wu got up and went into the shower. Once she heard the water gurgling in the bathroom she let out her first sob. She whimpered. Tears just poured out like spring water and couldn't be stopped.

In the bathroom Xu Wu also cried.

Enze Township is located at the most obscure place in south Zhejiang. It has been in existence for nearly a thousand years. Legend has it that when Emperor Qianlong of the Qing Dynasty made his tour to the south of the Yangtze River he had actually stopped here. And because a local girl was fortunate enough to have won his favor, the town was thus given the name Enze (literally "favor bestowed"). However, according to another version of the legend, the town was named after Emperor Qianlong's favorite concubine Enze who died on his tour of the South and was buried here, and that the town's name was changed in memory of her. There were still many other versions circulating at Enze. Xu Wu had heard them all as a child, but his father tended to believe the second version. His father was rather close to the owner of a gold shop who was many years his senior and the version was passed on to him through that owner. It was rumored that the shop owner made his fortune by buying gold and other jewelries from gravediggers.

In the end, Lin Zhuo decided to accompany Xu

Wu on his trip home. Enze was also the place they first met. Lin Zhuo was there on her senior class trip. The smiling young girls walking on the slate pavement immediately caught the eyes of the men in town, and Xu Wu was one of them. But he was home to pay respect to his mother's grave and intended only to make a short stay before going back to his work in Shanghai. He was twenty-five, three years after graduation from college he had already been promoted to the assistant engineer position. He liked Lin Zhuo from the first moment he set eyes on her because of her quiet demeanor. They asked him to take a picture for them, and he surreptitiously kept the camera focused on Lin Zhuo and lingered. He stared at her again and again until he saw signs of discomfort in her gaze. How come it's taking so long! Someone complained. Hearing that, he hurriedly pushed down the shutter. The picture was out of focus because he was too tense.

He later asked for Lin Zhuo's phone number. After coming back to Shanghai, he started his eager pursuit. He asked her out to eat, shop, to see a movie, play games and drink coffee. His work was definitely put on the back burner the first year they fell in love, as if they regretted that they hadn't known each other sooner. Lin Zhuo just started working that year and avoided field assignments as much as she could because she was in love. Two years later, when those who joined the company the same year as her were promoted to consultants, she remained an assistant consultant. But Lin Zhuo had no problem with that because having Xu Wu meant that she had it all. If bearing children or not was not an issue they should remain an ideal couple very much in love. For the last couple of years she had been doing rather well at her job. She was now in a position to have her own team to negotiate with clients. But just as she thought that her days would get better and better her marriage seemed to be heading for a crash inexorably.

They had been living separately for a long time. There were no words or physical affection. True, what is the point of keeping such a marriage, a marriage that produced no children?

At learning that his son was about to get a divorce, Xu Wu's father went silent for a long while. Finally, he slammed down his water pipe on the table and said no way! With his hands on his back, he went out the door. Xu Wu was stunned, so was Lin Zhuo. They glanced at each other and neither said a word. At nightfall, the old man brought home half a dozen bottles of aged osmanthus wine to share with his son. He got so drunk that he couldn't stand up straight. With blood-shot eyes and with obvious pain, he said:

You are not my son.

This is what happened. They had no children in the first dozen years of their marriage, not that there were no pregnancies, but the babies never lasted to full term. They later went to the county orphanage and adopted a boy, treating him like their own. But the mother of Xu Wu refused to let it go like that. She said that she would keep the bloodlines of the Xu family alive. And that was how a rather plump woman became drained and weakened by miscarriages and finally died of hemorrhage. For years Xu Wu's father blamed himself for what happened. After seeing the unpredictable nature of life and the hope of people for future lives at the crematory, what did he care about bloodlines? The words of his old friend, the gold shop owner, came to his mind: In your lifetime, you make do with what you have and never ask for more. If one cares too much about what others think, one might lose happiness for good.

You don't know that the shop owner was quite a womanizer back then. The old man was a little tipsy, he held up his glass and continued his story with his head swaying from side to side. When he was fifty years old, he fell in love with a girl who was retarded. He let his apprentices take care of the gold shop and became a mountebank, spending his days with the girl in the mountains looking for herbal medicine. There were also people saying that they were making out in the mountains! But who knows and who cares? The girl didn't live long. She died a few years later of tuberculosis. I handled the cremation of her body while he cried his heart out outside the crematory. Son, tell me what is love. Your old man understands that love is believing the one closest to you is forever the best. It doesn't matter whether she is retarded or not, whether she bears children for you or not. Your mother's death was so undeserved, so undeserved!

Xu Wu helped his rambling father to rest. He himself also had a little too much to drink. He had tears in his eyes. Lin Zhuo sat in the other room deep in thought. Faced with all the dishes and the left over half bottle of wine, she raised the glass and gulped down three in a row. She then threw herself on the table and cried uncontrollably. She had a hard time breathing, as if someone had rubbed and kneaded her heart repeatedly.

That night, Xu Wu and Lin Zhuo slipped into the same comforter. He didn't rush to have sex with her. Instead, enveloped by the sweet scent of osmanthus exuded from their bodies, they had a good night sleep. The next day, they took a leisure walk in town, holding hands just like when they first met. They talked, mostly about the little things that happened back in the days when they were deeply in love, and realized that the memories were still fresh for the both of them. Xu Wu made up his mind that to the young intern he could only offer his apology. At the tea house on the other side of the town they ran into an old person, who when setting his eyes on Lin Zhuo from afar pointedly walked over and offered to tell her fortune. Xu Wu thought he was a charlatan and tried to wave him away. No thanks. He now felt the need to cherish and protect his wife.

The old man to their surprise simply sat down and refused to leave. Upon seeing the gold ring on Lin Zhuo's left hand, the old man insisted to have her slipped it out of her finger so that he could have a look. Do you know what the inscription says? He murmured. Why wear such heavy stuff at such a tender age, young lady? He then copied the writing of the inscription and showed it to Lin Zhuo and Xu Wu in enlargement. *Pure Land Amitabha Mantra*. It turned out to be the mantra for the dead, something that should be worn by the dead, and the nectar is meant to eliminate the vile spawn. The old man shook his head. You should not wear this, you shouldn't.

After returning to Shanghai, Lin Zhuo and Xu Wu took the advice of the old man and place the gold ring near the statue of Buddha at the entrance of their apartment. One day, they both dreamt of the mother of Xu Wu mending clothes. She looked very young, in her early twenties. She was inspecting her husband's clothing when suddenly a gold ring rolled out from one of the pockets. She picked it up, liked it and put it on her finger.

A year and half later Lin Zhuo gave birth to a healthy baby boy. Xu Wu named him Xu Enji, expressing the hope to continue to have the favor bestowed.

The gold ring was indeed from one of the robbed graves, but there was no way to know for sure whose grave it was. Rumor had it that it was the grave of the favorite concubine of Emperor Qianlong, Enze. It was later sold to the gold shop owner. The owner at the age of fifty came to know the pregnant retarded girl who fell and miscarried right in front of the gold shop. He saved her life, used the ring as an IUD for her and took her in. He never knew the meaning of the inscription on the ring, never knew how to study it anyway. After the cremation of the girl, the father of Xu Wu found this peculiar ring in the ashes. He had wanted to return the ring to the shop owner, but the family was poor at the time and he had never bought anything significant for his wife. When the ring was found by his newly wedded wife and was put on her finger because she loved it, he decided to keep it as a gift for her. That was how the gold ring once used as an IUD device and had dead mantra inscribed on it was passed on to Lin Zhuo.

Xu Wu and Lin Zhuo didn't know the full story of the ring, however they didn't throw it away either, for it was the ring that led them to understand that a ring could always be replaced, but not love or the people close to you.

Old Grudge

Yanqing scraped the leftover rice from the bowl with the blue rim and gathered it in a small square garbage box. She never finished every grain of rice in her bowl and instructed her daughter Xianni early on to always leave something in the bowl, because only those who were starved in their previous lives would empty their rice bowls. And yet, she was by no means a wasteful person. The neatly folded square garbage boxes were made by her by using the supermarket specials that were stuffed in her mailbox. She also passed on all the housekeeping tips she learned from her mother to her daughter, and took this job of hers quite seriously too.

As to the habit of always leaving something in the rice bowl, she didn't learn it from her mother, that's for sure. But she could no longer recall where she got that idea from.

Xianni was sitting on the terrace under the sunshine, knitting from the ball of yarn from a bamboo basket, the dark green lamb's wool she selected from her mother's store at noon. She had pulled the collar of her white fleece cardigan up, her mouth closed tightly inside as if she was doing something that required extra effort. In fact, she had mastered all her mother Yanqing's knitting gestures, learned how to use the basket to hold the yarn, and putting rubber bands at the end of the bamboo needles. Yanqing used to scare her when she was young: "Mommy is knitting now, Xianni needs to behave, or you might go blind if your eyes are poked by the needles!" She would chuckle and wring a rubber band at the end of the needle as she said that. But obviously Xianni didn't really understand the role of the rubber band. She thought that whatever you do you had to get the posture right. Once you got that right, things would fall into place.

"So how are you getting along with Wu Boci?" Yanqing had finished washing the dishes, and was wiping her hands with a towel. She joined her daughter on the terrace, watching her knit. The autumn sun was very gentle. Tiny dusts and the good smell of the comforters (out to catch the sunshine) filled the alleyway. After only a few looks she couldn't help herself. "My goodness, your hand position is all wrong. How many times have I told you that your ring finger needs to hold the spare yarn or the tension of the stitches will be uneven?" She grabbed the needles from the hands of her daughter and shook her head after looking at the rows of knitting already done. With a disapproving sound coming out of her nose, she started to unravel the piece without uttering another word.

Before Xianni realized what had happened, her work was already mostly gone thanks to Yanqing. She pouted in the sunlight, betraying her displeasure. But ever since she was a child her mom had always acted that way and she was not allowed to go against mother's will. She unzipped her cardigan, letting out a sound of protest through the zipper. She stretched out her legs and her upper body as well before answering. "Just fine."

"Is this scarf for him?" Yanqing asked.

"No! It's for my own enjoyment!" Xianni became somewhat flustered. She hadn't finish stretching her upper body, turned her body a little to one side and almost lost her balance. She managed to awkwardly stand up. "Ok, mom, let me do it myself!" She took back the needles from Yanqing's hands as she said that.

"How come you never grow up? Are knitting needles toys for grabbing? You could poke yourself blind!" She complained, with the gesture of poking the needle to the eyes like she did when her daughter was a child. But with the sun shining above she could see clearly that her daughter was an adult now. The white fleece cardigan wrapped around her twenty-year-old body just right, her skin tone was fair and translucent, and the only blemish was the pinkish pimple on her left chin. Her elongated eyes were just like Yanqing's, and the shape of her face was more like her father when he was young.

"Mom, you should hurry to the store now. It's almost three o'clock!" Xianni held the needles in one hand and pushed Yanqing with the other. Her smile brought out two dimples at the corner of her lips and squeezed her two eyes into two curved lines, her most appealing look. Yanqing stumbled backward a little and with an outreached hand knocked on the forehead of her daughter twice before chuckling. Although her daughter was not very good with her hands, she could be playfully pleasant. Indeed, so long as you have the good looks no one will begrudge you for not being as smart.

"Oh, mom, I must have misplaced my house key. Can you leave me yours?" Xianni turned around and added with a shrug.

"How could you lose something as important as house keys? What would happen if someone else found your lost keys? We would have to change all the door locks." Yanqing was already on her way out and started to trace back her steps. She just couldn't stop her nagging. She became aware in the past few years that sometimes she had the habit of yammering.

"I told you I must have misplaced it, but it's not lost. I'm quite sure of it!" Xianni raised one hand to assure her mother. With knitted eyebrows she again nodded her head with force and added, "It's not lost!" It was then that Yanqing fished a key chain from her coin purse and put it on the end table. "Take good care of it! And go find your lost keys as soon as possible. Don't waste your time on knitting. The sun is too bright for your eyes and you can't do it right anyway!" She then glanced at herself in the full-length mirror attached on the armoire, straightened out her merino dress, felt the body-shaping T-shirt bought by her daughter, and checked again if the dark brown Peony brand shoes were a good match with her clothes. The sun's rays on the mirror got reflected on the floorboard, casting a strip of light. Yanqing suddenly felt dizzy. She shook her head, hoping to regain her sense of time, but instead just swiftly walked out of the door without thinking.

"Ok." Xianni responded. She carefully put the needles back through the loops. The scarf after being unraveled by Yanqing had only the wrinkled border part left. Xianni became upset. Mom was always like that. She had to meddle because she didn't think that her daughter could do anything right. She turned around with the intention of getting her mother to leave when the cell phone in her pocket started vibrating. It was Wu Boci. She realized that her mother was already gone when she answered the phone, but she hadn't heard her mother saying goodbye and closing the door.

"I got the keys." Xianni stood up, walked to the end table and picked up the key chain left by her mother. She put her left index finger in the ring and gave it a twirl. The clinking sound was meant for Wu Boci on the other end of the phone. "You can come over later and I will take you in."

It was only when she reached the end of the lane that Yanqing came half out of her daze. She felt that she was in a dream when she walked out of the door like a ghost, and she seemed to have passed several

neighbors downstairs without saying hello. She
wanted to respond to their question: "Have you had
lunch?" But somehow she couldn't utter a sound.

"Yanqing Yarn Store" was located across the street
from one end of the alleyway. Colorful yarns and several
sweaters Yanqing knitted and shawls she hooked were
on display behind the floor-length glass door that
covers half of the storefront. Yanqing was not fully
recovered. She walked towards the store in confusion.
The girl she asked to tend the store before lunch had
rushed to the entrance and said in soft Shanghainese
with a Suzhou accent: "Auntie Qing, you are here at
last. My boss is about to call me back to work." She went
back into the store, returned the account book and
money to Yanqing, grabbed a handful of melon seeds
on the counter and walked out in a hurry. Because she
sometimes had to cook lunch for her daughter Xianni,
Yanqing would ask the girl who worked at the hair
salon next door for temporary help and occasionally
gave her a couple of skeins of her lesser quality yarns
and free melon seeds as compensation.

Yanqing took a look at the book. Several boxes
of fleece wool, the kind Xianni chose for her scarf
project, were sold during lunch hour. As winter was
approaching, some young girls just loved to knit
scarves for their boyfriends. Yanqing would teach

the customers who were eager to learn how to knit gloves and hats for free. Back in the days when she was dating, knitting scarves was definitely not considered a sought-after skill, because all girls knew how to do it. Only gloves and hats were considered novel, because they were not as serious as sweaters, and yet they were small and exquisite and best to show off one's knitting skills. But the times have changed. Girls who were able to knit scarves from beginning to end had been in sharp decline, not to mention those who could knit gloves and hats.

Closing the book, Yanqing took out a half-finished light yellow merino wool turtleneck from under the counter and uttered an involuntary sigh. Why was she overcome by a sense of sadness? The knitting was not yet finished because it was very time-consuming for her to work on three strands together as the yarn was so thin. She knew it was going to be a time-consuming project and she started it anyway. She figured that it would take about two months, in time for Xianni to wear it when winter comes. At Yanqing's yarn store there was a box on top of the display shelf that contained all the wool clothing Xianni wore as a child. Yanqing didn't have the heart to unravel any of them. But now Xianni didn't like to wear wool clothing anymore. She complained that it irritated her skin and was uncomfortable. Yanqing's advice of wearing thermals underneath was met with a scathing retort. Only middle-aged women wore thermals!

That was why Yanqing chose to work on first-grade merino wool, an especially soft and gentle yarn that doesn't irritate the skin for her daughter's winter clothing. As to thermals, she also tried to ascertain from her daughter what they now wear underneath for winter. Detecting her mother's ignorance on matters like this, Xianni proudly replied: "Close-fitting T-shirts."

People of the older generation used to say that children were debts of the parents in their previous lives and when carrying into this life they were inescapable. Yanqing found this adage couldn't be truer today. She used to feel that her daughter, who looked just like her and had been a beauty loved by everyone ever since she was a child, was the work she was most proud of. She herself was the best-looking girl in the neighborhood when she was young and had high hopes for herself too. But she was not born at an auspicious time. She dropped out of school only after a few years and later married a workshop technician not necessarily by choice and had Xianni. After marriage, Yanqing and her husband were not the loving couple in the strict sense of the word, but they got along fine. Although her mother-in-law in Yangzhou had some reservations about Xianni for being a girl, she didn't wear it on her sleeve and took rather good care of Yanqing during her confinement. Her neighbors and relatives were all in agreement that Yanqing was fortunate to have married a good husband. She also shared that view once. But when Xianni was ten, her husband suddenly dropped dead at work after months of putting in overtime hours. Yanqing cried so hard on the bench outside the morgue that she fainted several times that day. She was blind-sided by the event. She had no idea why she was crying and what she felt so sad about. Her crying seemed to be mechanical, in a subdued whine. In her fainting spells she seemed to have seen the young woman who cried while holding a dead cat twenty years ago. She couldn't bear to hear her weeping which sounded creepy. She was twelve then. She hid herself behind the door, suppressing the throbbing heartbeats in her chest. It was she who fed the cat with fish tripe mixed with mouse poison, but she only meant to try out the formula dispensed by her school to eliminate the four pests. Was her story true? Was there any element of malice involved in the incident at all? She was too young at the time and wasn't sure. And after things went awry she was simply too terrified to dissect her motives, and was tormented by frightening dreams night after night.

At forty-two now, the two heart-wrenching scenes of ten and thirty years ago have mostly faded with age. It was after her husband's death that she discovered her daughter Xianni's resemblance to her father, and it was also after his passing that she realized that she never loved him. About a week after the funeral, Yanqing was able to stand before the full-length mirror to ponder what to wear to make her look her best. With one hand holding the school bag of her daughter Xianni, the other holding Xianni's arm, she whisked through the alleyway amid the whistles of a few young hoodlums. She seemed to enjoy the attention of others no matter who they were, to the point that she found the life of a single mother fashionably lonely.

After knitting a few rows, Yanqing suddenly remembered that she should have reminded Xianni not to lose her key chain as well. She instinctively wanted to go back home and tell her daughter what was on her mind, but her body for some unknown reason seemed a bit rigid. She calmed down and resumed her knitting only after fidgeting a little in her chair. Just let it go, she told herself and sighed.

Xianni saw Wu Boci coming her way from the terrace

and greeted him in a restrained voice. Wu Boci raised his head, had a painful look on his face when the glittering sun shone directly into his eyes. He leapt forward and ducked under the eave and Xianni burst out laughing as she leaned on the terrace door.

Xianni could no longer recall how they met. In fact, she never paid any attention to the presence of Wu Boci. It probably happened one evening after a summer storm when Xianni was sitting in front of her mother's store to catch some fresh air with her bare lower legs stretched out. She didn't seem to have any care in the world, even chuckled when seeing water splashed all around by the speeding cars passing by. Her demeanor and laugh caught the attention of Wu Boci from across the street. Yes, Xianni believed that it was that very evening that Wu Boci came into her life.

Every time Wu Boci and Xianni walked together as a pair they automatically became the object of envy; a beautiful girl next to a handsome young man. When they first set their eyes on Wu Boci, many neighbors were very impressed: "What an extraordinary pair!" And it was exactly for that reason that Yanqing implicitly sanctioned her twenty-year-old daughter's love interest for she enjoyed the whispers of those neighbors envious of her daughter's good fortune. Indeed, Boci seemed to be such a handsome, gentle and polite soul. Yanqing wanted to ask him about himself the few times he joined them for dinner, but the words simply would not come out. They were at the tip of her tongue and went back in at the last minute. And she was baffled by her own ineptness afterwards.

Xianni hid behind the door and listened with her ear at the door for the footsteps of Wu Boci, and yet he was the type who walked almost in silence. Today, Xianni faked the misplacement of her own key to get the key chain from her mother because she wanted to show Boci the south-facing room upstairs on the third floor, the room he always asked about. Xianni told him that it was a room occupied first by an old neighbor of her mother's family for at least ten years. Later another old couple whose son was in the United States moved in. A few years afterwards the son sent for them and they left the key for her mother in case of emergency. She never asked Boci why he was interested in that south-facing place. It seemed that she never asked him why from the moment she met him. Why did he like her? Why did he like to spend time with her? Why ... was she in love now? Xianni was a little confused. They held hands from time to time, but they were never intimate. Boci sometimes acted more like an older brother to her. His eyeballs were of a beautiful brown color, clutching Xianni in his always warm hands he walked with her in easy steps. Sometimes Xianni would leap up to swipe Boci's nose in a coquettish play. A touch of his damp and cold nose tip would send him into a sneezing frenzy. Sometimes Xianni, like other girls, couldn't help but fancy about what is to come for the two of them, but Boci would always act distracted.

As always, without Xianni detecting his footsteps he was already at the door knocking. Xianni quickly hid behind the door and opened it only slightly, ready to boo him when he stepped inside. But Wu Boci skillfully thwarted her scheme by pushing the door further in, stretching his hand behind the door and poked his head inside. This time it was Xianni who was caught by surprise.

"What happened to your eyes?" Xianni jumped out from behind the door and rushed to fetch a tissue from the end table. Wu Boci acted as if he only realized there was a problem after being reminded by Xianni. He walked towards the full-length mirror and saw the secretion of a yellowish brown color at the inner corner of his eyes. He reached for the tissue to wipe it out, paused a while and replied:

"It is probably caused by the glaring sun."

Getting the key, Xianni took Wu Boci's hand and went upstairs. There was a small iron gate with open grids at the quarter landing that had been given a fresh paint of dark green, with a khaki-colored linen curtain hung behind it. Xianni still remembered the old couple that lived here. When she was a child they often dropped by because they were lonely. They loved small children and urged Xianni to call them grandpa and grandma, and were overjoyed when she did.

"When did they move out?" Wu Boci asked. Xianni opened the iron gate and tried to dust off the curtain by whirling it in the air.

"When I was about eight or nine. When Dad passed away they even called from the United States to console Mom." Xianni groped for the light switch as she spoke. After being left vacant for more than ten years the place looked lifeless. Wu Boci couldn't help but sneezed again. He then used his two hands to cover his nose to ensure smooth breathing. The door to the south-facing apartment was the old-fashioned kind and was painted in the Kailin brand light brown color. The lock was rectangular in shape with a round knob. Since its core was no longer working, a cylinder lock was added underneath. Stooping a little, Xianni tried each key on her key chain. Wu Boci was standing

behind her with his hands constantly pressing his
eyes, overtaken by a sense of grief.

Yanqing was sitting at the yarn store knitting, rather
relaxed and reminiscing about things from the past.
But all of a sudden the dizzy feeling she had after lunch
returned. She felt that her two hands were slowly
becoming stiff and inflexible and she could no longer
hear the sounds of traffic from the street. She seemed
to have risen from her body and walked back home
without thinking, but not before turning around and
looking at herself knitting behind the counter.

Yanqing knew the alleyway like the back of her
hand. Late in the afternoon everyday, the neighbors
would start picking the vegetables right in front of
their homes. If they were having fish that day, the
small slate slabs of the alleyway would become their
chosen spots to scale the fish. In one similar evening
thirty years ago, she was coming back from school
that had just been reopened. She went through this
alleyway and as she was turning the corner, heard
the mother of the Zhang family in the next building
lecturing her son. Why are you eating so fast? Were
you always hungry in your previous life? Don't eat
it all up, leave some rice behind! The young Yanqing
peeked in a little and went into her building.

The stairs looked exactly as they were thirty years ago, with odd items from different families piled up in the stairwell here and there and baskets of preserved ham and dried foodstuff hanging in midair. The wooden stairway creaked under one's footsteps, occasionally surprising the mice hidden under the floorboard. Nobody was home. Xianni must have gone out. Yanqing felt that her own body was too eerily light, with just a slight move she turned around. There was a ray of light at where the stairs turned at an angle, a light that came from the south-facing apartment on the third floor. Yanqing slowly walked upstairs, as she did when she was about twelve years old. She suddenly remembered that she forgot her house key that evening, as it happened to her today. She was sitting on the steps staring in the air when the cat raised by the young lady living in the south-facing apartment started scratching the iron gate fence, making a piercing "huahua, huahua" noise. The young lady was about twenty-five or twenty-six. The whole building used to belong to her family. Then both her parents died in labor camps in the countryside, and according to people who lived in the building, she just snapped as a result and had only a Persian cat as her companion. Little Yanqing poked her head and took a closer look at the cat. It was a Persian cat with a light yellow fur and a flat face. It seemed friendly, but kept on scratching the iron gate and meowed. Are you hungry, kitty? She asked and used a finger to poke at the kitty's head. In the satchel resting on her knees there was a package of rat poison issued by the class hygiene officer who specifically instructed her to put the poison in an enamel dish in the stairwell.

Even today, Yanqing still couldn't figure out what had driven her to rush downstairs to fetch the tripe left behind by mother Zhang, mix it with the rat poison and feed it to the cat through the iron gate. As to the young lady, she did arouse her curiosity. At the time, little Yanqing didn't understand what loneliness meant. She only felt that she looked very sad the few times she appeared on the staircase. Neighbors whispered behind her back that she had snapped and she no doubt acted that way by shutting herself in her own world, talking only to her cat.

After the death of the Persian cat, for a while Yanqing waited for something to happen. She figured that probably the young lady would step out of the iron gate and talk to others. She actually liked the woman, because she was beautiful and had no issues with anyone. It was not easy to have no issues with anyone in those days. And yet to her surprise, the

woman died not long after her cat's demise. As to
how she met her end, there were different versions
circulating among the neighbors. Some claimed she
killed herself by slitting her wrist. Some said she died
of an overdose of sleeping pills. There were still others
who claimed that she died of a terminal disease. Later
when a new couple moved in to the south-facing
apartment, the rumors finally dissipated, to the point
that no one seemed to remember the young woman
anymore with the exception of Yanqing who held
herself partly responsible for her death. Absolute
isolation and grief could kill people.

Turning her way upward, Yanqing realized that
the door to the south-facing apartment was open,
and with her suspicion aroused she climbed the stairs.
Seeing the open doorway, Yanqing felt her eerily light
body suddenly froze and her heartbeat increased as she
saw the young lady and the Persian cat with light yellow
fur were both there. The young lady's face looked pale
and translucent. She held the cat in her bosom and
whispered, "You are finally back." Sadness disappeared
from her face, but the cat was crying. Because of their
short nasal passages the tears of this cat species were of a
yellowish brown color. The last ray of evening sun came
in from behind the young lady. Feeling dazed once
again, Yanqing seemed to see her daughter Xianni, and

it was her who was holding the cat.

After some struggling in her dream, Yanqing woke up. When her hand touched her ice-cold forehead she realized that it was covered with sweat. The sky outside the yarn store suddenly brightened up. It was not evening at all. It was then that Xianni came in with a bag.

"Mom, here is the close-fitting T-shirt you wanted." Xianni stuffed the bag into Yanqing's hands and took a few skeins of dark green lamb's wool from under the counter on her way out. "I'm going to need these for the scarf I am working on."

Shell Images

Liangyou once again heard Grandma scolding Mother. Grandma was sitting by the pile of grain, holding a rice bowl and was very much enjoying what she was doing. Curse words like "bitch" and "shit" were spewing out again and again, which was nothing new. She didn't expect Mother to talk back probably because she knew for sure that her daughter-in-law, soft as a ripe persimmon, would never utter a sound because she was a doormat. When Grandma became tired of scolding she started crying, and poked at the sun-dried grain with her feet at the same time.

Liangyou, lying low on the terrace, kept his watch on the sly. Mother was washing clothes on the cement slab by the well, a few meters behind the pile of grain that was making a scratching noise at the push of a pair of angry bound feet. In his grandmother's rice bowl there was still half of a cold, stiff wheat bun with pork filling left.

Hearing Grandma's crying, Mother washed her soapy hands in the lead pail and wiped them quickly on her apron. She then turned to sweep the grain with a broom, still without making a sound, so that the pile disturbed by grandma's feet could be restored to its original shape. Only that the pile had been moved further. Mother raised her head towards the sun, as if she was finding the exact location of it. She was trying to convey the message that the move was meant for the grain to go after light and warmth, and not to reconstruct what was destroyed or prevent it from being destroyed again.

Unfortunately, the moment Mother raised her head she noticed Liangyou in his hiding place. "Go do your homework right away!" She was about to speak when Liangyou took the words out of her mouth and scurried back to the room inside. He picked up a pencil on the desk and with the fastest speed solved an algebra problem. He then tried to listen to the goings-on downstairs. Grandma stopped scolding and started discussing with Mother what to eat for dinner.

This kind of drama has been commonplace in the years since his father's passing.

"Let's go, Ma Liangyou, another person will scale the chimney!" Guan Dongbao, wearing a new haircut, and several other boys of the same town, together with his younger sister Guan Chunni, came running to ask Liangyou to join them. As soon as the young teenagers showed up at the door, the black family mutt "Hua Mulan" started barking aimlessly, which alerted Grandma. She took out the half wheat bun from her rice bowl and gestured to chase the kids away.

"You bunch of mischievous kids! Why are you interested in watching scaling the chimney among all things? Go! Go away! Don't you drag—" Before she could finish her sentence, Liangyou bee-lined down the stiars clutching his homework. He took the leftover wheat bun from Grandma and tucked his homework into his mother's arms. "I finished it all!" Without waiting for any reply from anyone, he opened the yard gate and ran outside. As he was running out he also tried to stop Hua Mulan from following him, and threw it the leftover bun as a reward. "Be a nice dog! Go home!" He said.

Dongbao and Chunni were chortling, seemingly more eager than Liangyou to run to the scene.

"Scaling the chimney" was the local language used in south Zhejiang Province. It had nothing to do with anyone actually scaling the chimney. It was a reference to "incineration." At Lishui Township people who were bad with directions would rely on the high chimney of the incinerator at the crematory for help because it towered over all other buildings. The crematory was located at the northwest corner of the town. Once someone was being incinerated, white smoke would billow out of the stack, and the smoke would only appear towards evening hours. Every time, while watching the white smoke enveloped in steam against the setting sun to the west, Liangyou would believe that once the smoke drifted far and dissipated they would certainly reach the other side of the sky.

Liangyou appeared to have both faith and fancy in that kind of end to life, hence his regret at his father's being deprived of the opportunity to "scale the chimney."

Because of the strong objection of his grandma

his father was given a white cloud burial.

The so-called white cloud burial was to have the coffin in a small brick house on a level spot halfway up the mountain for several years before the actual burial. Legend has it that this was the custom passed on to the province after the southern move of the North Song Dynasty, because many people at the time believed that they could still go back home and were wishing that they could also take their family members home with them some day.

While Dongbao and the other kids were skipping stones across the turtle farm breeding pond, Liangyou dragged Chunni's clothes and asked her if she knew who was going to "scale the chimney" today. Chunni shook her head. "The adults were saying just now that he was a worker at the pig farm on the west side of town. He was there to feed the pigs, but was tripped by a sow in heat. The back of his head hit the slops trough and that was how he died." Liangyou pressed the tip of his nose and mimicked the sound of the sow. "A sow in heat is indeed a scary scene!" He then burst out laughing.

When Chunni finally got the joke she raised both of her arms in an attempt to hit him.

"The sow is pushing her way around!" Liangyou

screamed. After playing with each other for a while they realized that other kids, totally ignoring them, had all stopped their game and stooped by the pond, staring. Chunni ran to them, hovered around her older brother and gazed at the pond. She was immediately hooked and became motionless. Liangyou walked over and joined in the observation. Their backs lined up along the edge of the pond, with the flattened stones that they selected for the game piled by their side. White smoke were billowing out of the stack towering over the northwest sky, drifting away with the wind and dispersing, reaching the other end of the sky like Liangyou had imagined.

The scene in the farm pond had never been seen by Liangyou, Dongbao or Chunni, the kids who had lived at Lishui for over a decade. For most, it was probably a first even for people like their mothers and grandmas who had spent their whole lives here or had lived here for generations.

Grandma and Mother had clashed many times over whether the body of his father should be incinerated or given a white cloud burial. The clashes had all been transformed into Grandma's cursing in the memory of Liangyou before he reached the age of ten. In the end, Mother turned mum and his father was given the white cloud burial. Going back even further, Liangyou's only memory of his father took place at a temple fair when he was five. He had insisted on sitting on his father's shoulders during the fair tour, but was hurt by the poking shoulder blades of his thin-frame after a short while. The constant pain in his behind drove him into unrestrained crying. Hearing him, Mother came running through the crowd and got him down from his father's shoulders. Liangyou turned towards his father and he saw through his tears a face that looked awkward, resigned and even embarrassed. He had always been in poor health. He looked pale and wasted.

Looking back now, he believed that his mother's removing him from his father's shoulders meant more than the move itself. The term "father" was only a pronoun to him now. It existed in the stories given by Grandma and Mother. There were, of course, also pictures and the little brick house on a flat land halfway up the mountain slope. Every time he accompanied Mother to visit the grave he would stare blankly at the small brick house with no doors or windows where his father was lying inside. He would burn ritual money and mock ingots for his father; offer him apples, bananas and wheat buns. He would kowtow to his father, getting a lot of dirt

on his forehead and then stand by stiffly, listening to
his mother's crying. In contrast to his grandma, his
mother was not as prone to crying, but the sounds of
their crying were quite similar for whatever reason.

Liangyou found the sound unpleasant, even
chilling.

"The townspeople are saying that the new county
government is against white cloud burials because
they take up too much land and that only incineration
would be allowed from now on! But Grandma is not
going to cooperate. She's resorted to scolding and
cursing again." This was his mother's latest complaint
to his father. She never felt the need to hide anything
because of Liangyou's presence and never really
needed his father to do her justice. Rather, her filing
of complaints seemed a continuation of their love. "I
really miss you, and so does Liangyou." She always
ended her talk with these words.

Hearing these words Liangyou knew that they
were now ready to go down. He watched his own
shadow cast on the ground and noted that it was
getting a little longer. He had really shot up fast in
the last few years, although Dongbao said that the
length of one's shadow may vary according to the
position of the sun and was unrelated to one's actual
height, he could see clearly that the shadow that

couldn't even reach the little brick house before was now making contact with it. Liangyou moved his feet a little without thinking so as to move his shadow out of the brick house. He remembered that Grandma's grievance against his mother seemed to have something to do with shadows.

The traditional white could burial requires that the deceased, before being put into the coffin, be carefully shaded from light and kept at a distance from people and more importantly, that one should never allow shadows to be cast on the coffin; or the one who cast the shadow will be cursed with life-long misfortunes. But Liangyou at the time was too young to know about the rules. In a long, white mourning garment, he stood on the tip of his toes in an effort to see his father being put into the coffin. Grandma uttered a cry of surprise as Liangyou's shadow cast on the coffin. Grandma with her bound feet immediately grabbed him in her arms and walked towards the door. Liangyou was stunned. Now tightly clasped in Grandma's arms, his head was soon dunked in a lead pail by the well. His whole face was prickled by the icy cold well water. Liangyou had a high fever the next day, but Grandma seemed happy. She said that the fever would undo the curse.

On their way down Liangyou asked his mother,

"What did my father look like? I would like to have a picture of him."

The secret discovered by Liangyou and Dongbao in the farm pond soon spread all over the town of Lishui, because kids are the worst keepers of secret among all human beings. Every day they would bring one more kid to the edge of the pond to look. When more and more people got involved, more and more people knew about the secret. Adults knew, old people knew, men knew, and women knew too. People arrived at the pond in succession to explore the things that looked like faces of human beings under the water. Some tried to poke the faces with dead tree limbs, and the faces moved under water. It turned out that they were not ghosts, but turtle shells.

People recognized the faces of their deceased father, mother, friend, relative, teacher, neighbor, and even the face that belonged to the old mayor of the town. Their features were etched eerily on the turtle shells in light grey. They fished the turtles out for a closer look and found nothing unusual except the images on the shell. But Liangyou never found a face that matched the picture of his father. Grandma and Mother later also joined in the search. They were hoping that they could, as the other townspeople, buy back the faces of their loved ones. But not everyone had their wishes granted. They discovered that the faces of those who died earlier could not be found. Missing also were those who were buried or given the white cloud burial. Only faces of those who passed away recently and scaled the chimney could be found.

It was then that Grandma agreed to the county request to switch from white cloud burial to cremation. She felt that once the body was cremated the soul would settle in the shell, and she could then take her son back home. Her son was not gone, he still existed, only in a different form.

Unlike direct burial, several years after the white cloud burial the body of the deceased still needs to be buried into the earth. In other words, it uses the precious land twice. The county has long wanted to change this local custom and promote cremation. They definitely didn't expect that their "project" could be carried out so successfully without a hitch here in Lishui Township.

The day his father was sent to "scale the chimney" Grandma cried the hardest in her life. Liangyou saw that the coffin taken out of the small brick house was already rotten. The takers then put it in a larger coffin, dexterously closed the lid, and marched towards the smokestack. The ceremony seemed hasty in comparison with the white cloud burial earlier. Liangyou was old enough now to commit every detail to his memory. He walked behind the pall bearers, along with Grandma, Mother, and Hua Mulan. He felt that the coffin was not heavy, since his father inside was mostly gone.

That very same day Grandma mentioned out of the blue that Gu Yanwu wrote in his book *Geography and Customs of the Ming Dynasty* that there were eight backward customs practiced in the town of Lishui and that cremation was one of them, since only the barbarian Qiang people would burn the dead body and let the ash be blown away. It turned out that she received several years of education in an old-style private school before her getting married, and as she aged she tended to cling hard to whatever she learned in her youth. That was the general rule; as you age you tend to retain what you learned long ago and not what happened recently. Liangyou stood outside the crematory and watched the white cloud billowing from the smokestack with the thinning smoke disappearing towards the other end of the sky.

A few days later holding a heavy urn in both his arms he cried his way home, as Dongbao, Chunni, and others watched. Both his mother and grandma told him that he had to cry hard, the louder the better. He imitated the bawling sound of Grandma and Mother. He felt that he wouldn't be able to feel the cold if he cried as hard as he could.

The bawling sound only succeeded in sending chills through the listeners.

Later, the pond of the turtle farm was gradually abandoned. Grandma and Mother never got the shell that resembled his father. One day, Dongbao and his friends found out that the owner of the farm had disappeared, and a few days afterwards people from the county government showed up and took away the owner of the crematory; the turtles that were taken home couldn't even survive the winter of the south and they died soon afterwards.

It was much later that it was reported on the web that turtles loved bone ashes, so people were buying ashes from the crematory to feed the turtle. This was one of the weird news stories that Liangyou read about.

The Night of Rammasun

I always wanted to give a complete story of an event about a number of people; a story of true, reliable and not made-up event and flesh and blood people. It proved to be a fairly difficult job, because when describing it in the first or the third person, I had a tendency of getting the sequences mixed up and changing the people beyond recognition that it became fiction.

Once again, I began to tell my story. You were sitting in my room and it was pouring outside, I handed you a towel. If not for having no other place to duck from the rain, you probably would not agree to listen to my story, right? Others often complained that my fictionalization went too far and that my characters and plots were unbelievable, even absurd.

So far, no one had been able to sit through my story, which was really frustrating and also added to my anxiety.

I can assure you that this time I will rein in my imagination and tell the story only by unlocking my memory.

Dashan.

As to his name, for easy memory let's call him Dashan. Actually, that was what everybody called him many years ago. As to his height and weight, when I saw him two years ago he was about six feet tall and weighed about eighty kilograms. There was stubble on his chin, he wore a crew cut, and there was an unremarkable mole on his right cheek, a mole that was discernible only up close. Its existence came to my notice only because Onetwo had told me that she had her eyes open when they kissed.

She discovered the mole that was indiscernible to others without even trying.

The near-unanimous opinion was that those who kissed with their eyes open should not be believed, because it showed that their feelings were not sincere.

I agreed with the first point and disagreed with the second, what about you?

Onetwo.

As to Onetwo, there is so much to tell that days, nights or even months would hardly be enough. We had been together from the days when we shared the use of the kitchen in the old apartment complex, and we used to grab fistfuls of popped fava beans in bright green to fill our lunch bags which had the words "keep our places clean" printed on the outside. Her last name was Four, as in "one two three four," and her first name was Onetwo, as in "one two three four." Don't jump to the conclusion that her parents was illiterate or semi-illiterate, a legacy of the Cultural Revolution. She was given the name because her parents' wedding anniversary fell on the twelfth of April (the fourth month of the year) in the 1970s.

As for Dashan, I could use the excuse of not having seen him for two years to be vague about his exact features. But I couldn't do that to Onetwo, because we looked increasingly alike as we practically grew up right next to each other.

I was thinking whether I should go back to the very beginning—many, many years ago—to start my story. You thrust the towel back to me and asked me to continue, you also told me that I had in fact started telling the story, only that I was not aware of it.

You made a friendly gesture of closing the window at the other end of the room for me, a typhoon was supposed to hit us tonight.

You took the CD out from your waistband, I could tell that you must have selected it carefully from a huge pile of pirated CDs offered on the street, but I still wondered why there were street hawkers willing to do business in this pouring rain and why there were customers like you. Muscles with droplets of water came into my sight, quite unexpectedly, and my eyes just lingered.

A CD by Sarah Brightman. You complained that I should have a Hi-fi system of a better quality.

Let me continue with my story as the music plays.

I cuddled next to you on the sofa. Your hair was still a little wet and sticky. Our noses touched one another.

Did you get a good look at me, aside from the eyebrows, and this was basically how Onetwo looked—no, lips should also be excluded; hers were not as dry as mine. She had dark and slim eyebrows and her other facial features were unremarkable. She didn't have big alluring eyes, nor did she have a big ugly nose or a big voluptuous mouth.

When the song *This Love* was played on the CD you started kissing me. Why? Was it because I just said that my lips were dry?

No, you should have stopped, wasn't I in the middle of telling you a story and you were listening?

There was a dip on the forehead of Onetwo, look, so do I.

When we were small we used to run around in

the kitchen and one day, by common accord, bumped our heads into the wooden kitchen door at the same time. That was how we both got the very fashionable "w" sign on the forehead, and when the "w" receded we were left with the dips. Don't laugh, it was after that that all our neighbors realized that we have grown more and more alike.

The parents of Onetwo were among post-Cultural Revolution college students recruited from workers, peasants and soldiers. So were mine, but this was something you knew already.

I must select an age to start my storytelling and not just making introductions. Where should I begin? Let's begin from the spring they met, and how many years ago was that? There is no need to be exact on that.

Some of those who had tried to listen to my story before chose to leave at this point out of boredom. I beg you not to do that. Do we have a deal?

It was in April of that year that I first noticed the name Dashan appearing on the letter from Onetwo, although I could no longer recall if it happened exactly on the twelfth, a date Onetwo claimed she was very sure about. Onetwo and I had been in regular contact through correspondence ever since we moved out of the old complex.

Give me some time to think of the exact words she used.

Dashan, my man.

Hmm. Yes, this was her opening sentence. You looked at me in disbelief, don't you trust me? I walked towards the desk, in a secret compartment of the desk drawer where there was a large craft paper envelope, you could probably guess what was inside. Yes, if you still harbored any doubt, I could find the letter and read it to you.

"Dashan, my man ...

"He said he loved me. I said if you were not a murderer I would marry you. He is much taller than I am, and much heavier too. He has two protruding teeth like the voles that make him look especially cute when he smiles. There is a black mole on his right cheek that I discovered when we kissed. He lured me by swearing his love for me to God, which is very special ...

"On the twelfth of April I decided to be with him. He agreed it is a good date.

"He gave me a Rado watch as a testimony of our love. Yes, he used the word love and I believe him.

"Onetwo, April 12, 1998"

You see, I didn't get it wrong. The letter is sufficient proof of the existence of Dashan and Onetwo. Onetwo didn't get the date wrong either. It was the twelfth of April. Although later she insisted that their anniversary fell on a different date.

And the black Rado watch later became evidence. Onetwo mentioned in her last letter. Sorry, we should proceed with our story in a chronological order and not jump around. I will get to that part of the story later.

The mother of Onetwo, whom I called Mother Four, died at the old complex. Father Four held her body throughout the night. Onetwo curled up in one corner and remained motionless the whole night. She said she was afraid of corpses, no matter whom it belongs to in life. At the time, Father Four was merely a section chief in the government bureaucracy, who didn't have much money and hospital care needed money. Actually, none of those who lived in that old apartment complex were well off. Very few people were rich in those days.

In fact, rich people are still few in number even today. Did you see the occasional expensive cars on the road? Father Four later owned one just like that. On the other hand, if you look at me, I have only one stereo system, the one you constantly complain about. But of course I am still sitting here in front of you, whereas he had been taken away with his hands cuffed in the back.

Two years after the death of Mother Four, Father Four was catapulted to the position of a bureau chief. And in less than a year he, along with Onetwo, moved out of the old complex, so we started our correspondence.

You started kissing me again. Your hair was half dry. The sky outside grew dark; I think the name of the typhoon was Rammasun. Kiss me if you want. This is how Onetwo described the kiss of Danshan, I would read it to you:

"He always lowers his head, wears a sly smile on his face and shamelessly sticks his tongue out. I like his way in general, but the thought that he could be more romantic did hit me once in a while, however, I am sure his response to that will be, 'To hell with it, I don't care.' It seems a bit rude. This man."

Dashan would kiss Onetwo anywhere, anytime, in the presence of me or any stranger. Whereas you, you would only kiss me when no one else is present. I am not complaining, nor am I making any comparison, but what am I doing?

Do you know that movie that starred Shirley Temple? You must remember it. I think the name of it is *The Little Princess*. There was a snobby principal, a dark-skinned Indian and a rambunctious monkey who perched on the attic and brought gifts to her with a smile on New Year's Day.

After the assets of her family were seized and forfeited to the government, Onetwo was left with nothing. All those who used to address her as "the invaluable (one thousand pieces of gold) daughter of the Bureau Chief" all disappeared from the scene.

Onetwo moved in with me, you see, we once sat on the same sofa and listened to music. At the time we hadn't met; at the time Dashan was still asking around for the whereabouts of Onetwo. In this room we listened to music all day long, but I really can't recall the names of the singers, the composers, or the pianists. Onetwo used a hairpin to secure her long bangs back and exposed the dip on her forehead. Snickering, she would ask me, "Look, it is still here, what about yours?"

Later, with her long fingernails, she parted the hair away from my forehead, felt the dip with her fingertip and said, "Your forehead is always so cold, even when you were a child."

You moved your lips away from my cheeks, parted my hair with your fingers. Is it here?

I nodded. Right there, a very obvious dip, and

that was why Onetwo and I both chose to wear long bangs in an attempt to cover the cost of our reckless past. Let me think, what was our exact posture as we hit the kitchen door? No, it seems my memory of how it happened was a little different. Onetwo must have pushed me when I hit it. Did we get into an argument before then over one piece of popped fava bean? Afterwards, she also banged her head against the door and we burst into laughter and cried. Onetwo was like that. She would punish herself the same way ever since she was a child.

The father of Dashan was an executive at a subsidiary enterprise of the bureau where Father Four was the chief. Onetwo and Dashan came to know each other at one of the regular visits between the two families. I am afraid I am not in a position to give you a full account in detail.

You nodded, pointing at that outsized craft paper envelope.

I searched for a long while and I couldn't find the letter in which Onetwo described their first meeting—a letter that existed in my memory. In order to make you believe its existence, I resorted to lying. Faking an honest look, I took out a letter dated close enough to their first meeting. Taking a chair and sitting across from you, I started reading.

Please pardon me for the lie. Some of those who listened to my story before refused to believe in me at this juncture just because I couldn't produce the reliable evidence. They waved their hands in disbelief, pushed me aside impatiently and left.

I firmly believe that if the letter existed, it must go like this:

"... At meal time Uncle Bai showed up with his son and told us to call him Dashan, because that was the name he was known by a lot of people. Uncle Bai arranged to have him sit by me, but my father told them that the seat next to me was always reserved for my mother. I saw that Uncle Bai was not at all pleased. Looking at my father sideways, the man named Dashan smiled and took a quick glance at me. I stomped him hard from under the table because I resented his mocking expression. I know he was mocking at the blind devotion of my father, yes, that was blind devotion. But aside from the movement of his lips he betrayed no other emotions. It seems that my stomping failed to have a deterrent effect, except that he was no longer smiling ..."

If it was Onetwo who described the scene, that would have been the tone she used. If someone mocked her father she was sure to teach that someone a lesson without any hesitation. But the mother of Dashan should also be there as well. Oh, I failed to include her in my creative writing. Just forget it and ignore her. It seems that in Onetwo's own version she only mentioned his father and never made reference of his mother.

According to Onetwo's logic, whatever she didn't have, neither should others.

Mother was a case in point.

I folded the fake letter, put it back in the envelope, together with the rest of the notes and letters.

You stood up, walked towards me, held me in your arms from behind me and started kissing my neck. There were signs of a typhoon coming. The trees below were shaking violently from one side to the other, and raindrops were splattering on the windows. I could hear the window shelves creaking in real.

You see, I too lost my mother and my father. Maybe that was why Onetwo took me in as her best friend. No, I shouldn't have said that. The basis of my friendship with Onetwo had been so altered by my imagination. Alas, what was I saying? I pushed you back to the sofa, you should sit there and seriously listen until I am through with the story, because I have tried so many times and have never succeeded in telling the story like it is towards its end.

You nodded, somewhat frustrated.

I was really worried that at this point of the story you, like the others, would throw away my arms in anger, tell me to stop my creative thinking, and demand that we should instead kiss and make love, listen to beautiful music, and let me be kissed softly by you and quit talking. Fortunately, you didn't act that way, you were just a little frustrated. You were not to blame; I have truly dragged the story too long. But I was merely trying to tell you the complete story in its original form, should I continue?

You lit a cigarette left on the coffee table and started smoking without even looking at me. When I hit it off with my bare hand, you were stunned, staring at me with your eyes wide open.

I crouched in front of you and gently caressed your surprised expression with my hands.

That was the way Onetwo hit off the cigarette of Dashan and this is what happened.

"The minute Dashan lit a 555 cigarette I smashed it off his hand. How could he smoke in the house? Even if father was not in he could always tell the smattering of the leftover air of burning tobacco. No one was allowed to smoke at home. He himself quit smoking after mother died. Nobody ever said that her lung cancer was definitely caused by smoking, or was related to his smoking. But that was how he saw things.

"Dashan went into a rage because of that. He said, 'Lady, no one ever dared to smash the cigarette off my hand. Now pick it up for me!'

"I was looking around for air freshener.

"He angrily squatted down and looked for his 555 around the sofa."

I forgot to tell you that Mother Four died of lung cancer. Father Four was a heavy smoker before. The cheap Flying Horse brand of cigarettes was his choice. The pack's cover showing a flying horse against the blue sky could always be seen from his half-transparent shirt pocket.

After Mother Four died, he insisted that his long years of smoking resulted in her dying of second-hand smoke.

After that, the flying horse and the blue sky were gone for good and in its place was a plastic case the size of a work ID. Onetwo told me that the case contained the marriage photo of her father and mother.

Onetwo said that was blind devotion, yes, I agree with her.

Roars of thunder could be heard outside. You asked

me if I have taken the flowerpots in from the terrace.

Of course, the pot of houseleek was Onetwo's favorite; it was a gift from Dashan. When she moved in with me she came in with a leather suitcase in tow and this pot of plant in her hand.

We didn't know who was the whistleblower behind the long letter with the opening phrase "I want justice."

Onetwo later on insisted that it must be the father of Dashan.

I saw a glimpse of doubt flashed in your eyes, but I didn't respond to it, and you didn't elaborate either, right? I will continue with my story and you might as well set aside your doubt for the time being.

The windows started shaking very hard. The wind that made its way in through the glass sounded like the howling of a ghost for justice. Don't you agree that this Rammasun was really a powerful typhoon? I love typhoons, so did Onetwo.

I might as well empty all the letters from the craft paper envelop on the coffee table. I have numbered them all, I will show you.

"Today the number three typhoon made its landfall. Dashan and I took the opportunity to break the glass front of a self-help hot pot store. The security people came out from the back, grabbed Dashan and wouldn't let go. Dashan told them that his name was Bai Dashan and he also cast a knowing smile at the store manager. They then let him go, because it was his father's store. He told me that his father was working on a huge project.

"It was raining cats and dogs. I asked him, 'How would you react to a lightening if it strikes now?' He said he would certainly take it head on to save me from harm, he also asked if his doing so would be considered a chivalrous act. I shook my head, that was merely a claim he made, who knows what really would happen in that scenario. Amid real lightening, he swore to god that if he wasn't telling the truth he would rather be struck by lightning.

"As is known to all, lightening is always followed by claps of thunder.

"He became anxious and kept on insisting that he would definitely stand between the lightening and me.

"I took his hand and started to run. I said, 'There is no need for you to take the brunt for me. We should try to flee, and that is the correct answer we are looking for.'"

Both Onetwo and I were especially excited about natural disasters. Does anyone still remember the earthquake that happened over a decade ago? Both Onetwo and I were wrapped in terry coverlets by our respective parents and immediately taken out of the old complex building. Not yet steady on our steps, we managed to free ourselves from the coverlet and giggled in excitement, to the surprise of the adults around us.

After the aftershocks, we both found in our apartments chunks of lime falling from the ceiling on the cement floor and each saved one in secret. We didn't consciously save them as part of our collection, we only felt that they looked interesting and should be saved, much like the cellophane candy wrappings collected by little kids. We only discovered many years later that the other person also had a chunk of ceiling lime for keepsake.

At that time, both our families occupied the ground floor, and families on the same floor all share the use of the kitchen and the bathroom.

Ferocious water that surges in thunderstorms and heavy rains would submerge the whole first floor in no time. It was what the adults called "high-tide water." Onetwo and I crawling on the same bed would get extremely excited in seeing the steel wash basin and the red plastic tub floating around in this tide water, and in seeing the grown-ups hard at work to bail out the water. We were very happy and even came up with the idea of sitting in a tub and let the water take us wherever it may go, but the tub capsized at the weight of Onetwo, who was rather fat. We ended up gulping in mouthfuls of rainwater and getting scathing lectures from the adults.

Our two families always got along very well. That was also the reason why when Father Four was promoted to be the bureau chief my father was able to get the position as his secretary, only that my father died with my mother three years ago.

That was why I apologized just now. In fact, the friendship between Onetwo and me was shaped in our formative years and it had nothing to do with the fact that I was alone and by myself.

I had been living at this place ever since they passed away. The rent here was reasonable, plus I also came into two sets of handsome insurance money. They died in their sleep of a gas leak from aging gas lines.

You lifted me up from the floor. I wasn't upset, really, very few people have sat through my story up to this point, and you were so full of sympathy for me. You kissed me right after I took a pause in my monologue. The wind gust outside had gained force and I could hear the crackling sound of tree limbs broken from downstairs, mixed with roars of thunder and the ruthless rattling of windows by raindrops.

Can you stop for a while? I intend to finish my story tonight and my hope is that you can hear me out.

With your frustration gone, you calmly allowed me to rest on your shoulders. From the slight movement of your shoulders I could count your heartbeat. You said that the forecasters predicted that the typhoon would stay only one night and that it would be a sunny day tomorrow with no rain. Yes, I had the name of the typhoon stored in my memory: Rammasun. Can you hear me finish the story tonight?

I continued to crouch by the coffee table and selected letters from Onetwo to read to you. There wouldn't be that many, because the fact is one month after she and Dashan smashed the window front of the hot pot store, Father Four was taken away by the authorities.

"I am now writing to you in the waiting room of the detention center. I am sorry that I hung up on you the other day. I didn't know how to put it in words and I had lost all my sense of direction. They say that my father not only took bribes and embezzled money, but the amount involved was also huge. My God, he was supposed to be promoted soon. My God, only last week my father was telling me that the project submitted by Dashan's father would be approved, because he would probably become the father-in-law to my husband.

"That is why when I accepted Dashan's gift of houseleek I told him that I am ready for marriage.

"And little did I expect that today I would be sitting at this lousy place waiting for them to let my father out to meet with me. This is not real. On my way here just now I almost begged all passersby to slap my face, so that I could immediately wake up and find myself lying in bed in my own room or in the arms of Dashan. But they ignored my plea as if it was a plea made by a total moron. The only thing left for me to do was to ask for paper and pen to write to you while waiting. I am really at a loss as to what to do."

I turned the letter towards you. Can you see the handwriting? The unevenness of the handwriting shows that she was so terrorized and scared that her hand couldn't hold the pen steady, hence the crooked handwriting. She wrote the letter in the waiting room of the detention center. After so many people thought her to be insane, this was the only way she could think of right away to vent her frustration. The letter was not finished. It stopped midway. I think it stopped when Father Four was led out.

You were attentive to details and noticed that

there was no stamp on the envelope. Yes, the letter was hand delivered by Onetwo herself, together with her luggage and the houseleek plant. Even her cell phone was confiscated. I know that Dashan had been trying to locate her. He phoned many times here and asked if I had heard from Onetwo. I told him no and that she even hung up on me the other day.

Onetwo knocked on my door, came in, sat on this sofa and put the houseleek pot carefully on the coffee table. No trace of tears on her face. Instead, she seemed to be in good spirit. She then took out her clothes from the leather suitcase and hung them in my closet. Then she went into the bathroom without saying a word. I stood by my window and started watching the raindrops. Yes, it was also a rainy day. You know, this place rains almost year round.

When I heard sobbing from the bathroom, I was full of self-reproach.

I selected a CD by Frye and Onetwo took out a black notebook. On the calendar insert she pointed out the trial date of her father to me, a date circled in black by a hybrid pen. I told her that Dashan had been looking for her many times and asked me to make sure that she would call him right away. Onetwo threw herself into my arms. Her hair was still wet. I could feel that a large area of my pajama became wet;

the aroma of her shampoo was all over me.

She said no and that I shouldn't tell anyone that she was here. This time, I finally saw water drops on her cheeks. I wasn't sure if they were leftover steam from the bathroom or tears. She then stood up with the houseleek in hand and asked me if there was a spot on the terrace with limited sun exposure. She said that Dashan told her that the plant didn't do well under prolonged sun exposure.

I felt your hair with my hands and it was now completely dry. The rain outside was getting increasingly ferocious. From time to time, there were also noises of things falling down from above, and of bamboo poles clashing against each other. Somewhat worried, you walked towards the window, and with your hands on the sash, you asked me when the clay walls were replaced and could they withstand the force of the typhoon blowing all night. I actually didn't know. The landlord only said that the place was earthquake and thunder proof, but he didn't say whether it was typhoon proof. Let it be proved tonight.

I again arranged the letters on the table in the order of their numbers and stuffed them back to the craft paper envelop. I left one letter out, you returned to sit on the sofa and held me tight by my waist. Will you be finishing your story soon?

Yes, we will be coming to the end soon.

I showed you the envelope and you stretched your neck a bit and said that this one had no stamp on it either.

You are right; this was the last letter Onetwo wrote me.

Onetwo lived here for six months. It was during those six months that Father Four passed away. As the deceased was committed to prison for serious offenses, his family was not allowed to collect his body. Onetwo went back to our old complex where new occupants had moved in long ago. On the night of the fifth seven-day period (thirty-five days) after the death of her father, she laid straw bales and fake gold ingots from the lane entrance all the way to the entrance of her old residence.

Some of our old neighbors still lived there. They were familiar with Onetwo and me, the two kids carrying the lunch bags emblazoned with the words "keep our places clean." Some kind-hearted people open the kitchen door for us and allowed us to wait inside until midnight. They also asked us to keep our voices low. After all, we were no longer residents here and there were people who consider the matter inauspicious.

After midnight, we started to look for the bales of straw and gold ingots we placed in corners around evening time. Onetwo took a lighter from her pocket and ignited them one by one. I knew that she learned these rites from her father. More than ten years ago, she was following Father Four when he lit the points of light and every time a light was lit he would say in a whisper, "You are coming home."

That night, Onetwo, my parents and I were accompanying Father Four all the way. Father Four told us that we should not look back or Mother Four would be scared, and once her soul was scared away she would not be able to come back home.

On the night commemorating Father Four's fifth seven-day period, on a small table in the kitchen—we all realized later that that was the table on which we used to have our meals, a table that was now covered in stain and grease—stood an empty urn with Father Four's picture stuck on top and a stack of tinfoil by its side.

I held Onetwo's hand in mine when we walked back and every time she lit a point of light she would whisper, "Dad, you are coming home."

I knew that she firmly believed that if the soul

truly existed Father Four would certainly come back here.

The last stretch of road, thinking back even today, seemed very long. Holding hands with Onetwo, that was how we grew up, I seemed to return to the night more than ten years ago. There were a lot of people walking with us then, but only Onetwo and I were here this time, all the others were dead. The last letter from Onetwo had put it this way. Sorry, I was overly anxious, just wait a minute, and I will soon read that letter to you.

After we finished lighting all the points of light, we waited in silence in the kitchen for the so-called soul to come home. Superstition has it that half an hour after finishing with the points of lights, the one closest to the deceased should lightly touch the urn with tinfoil, and if it sticks on even after you let go of your hand, it is a sign that the deceased is back with his soul to meet with his relatives.

It is actually just a common phenomenon in physics and both Onetwo and I knew it well.

But Onetwo still took out one paper after another in earnest and touched it against the urn. None of them stuck on. It seemed like the simple physics phenomenon was playing a small trick with Onetwo, the daughter who chose to ditch her belief in science. But if you could see the expression of Onetwo then, you would surely agree that the trick had truly gone too far.

The night more than ten years ago again came to mind. Father Four also arranged a setting like this, but he succeeded in having the tinfoil stick on the urn of Mother Four on his fourth touching. Father Four threw himself in front of the urn and began to cry. That was the first time I heard a man cry, a deeply touching and heart-wrenching cry. As to my parents, they were sitting on the side wiping away tears. Crouched in one corner, Onetwo and I were staring at the scene in stupidity. I was surprised that I merely remembered the crying of Father Four whereas Onetwo had recorded the whole process.

Onetwo tried the whole night, maybe it was her sweaty palm or something, but she never succeeded in having any tinfoil stick on the empty urn. According to superstition, the tinfoil would automatically fall after three in the morning the next day, when the soul of the deceased would follow the black and white impermanence (two messengers of the king of hell) to the nether world and would not return home anymore.

On the night commemorating the fifth seven-day period, the tinfoil indeed fell off the urn after three in the morning. Father Four chased it outside, knelt down at the gate and broke down in uncontrollable grief.

After three in the morning, Onetwo could no longer suppress her emotions and finally burst out crying. She cried so hard and so loud, I knew she must have disturbed our neighbors in their sleep, but I didn't try to stop her. I hated myself at the time for caring.

I only learned much later that Onetwo lied, and the father of Dashan landed in jail because of her lies.

She firmly believed that the father of Dashan was the whistleblower who wrote the letter to the authorities.

In court she pointed at the black Rado watch and told the judge, "It was a gift from Uncle Bai to my father, hoping that my father could help him out. Since it suited me well, Father just let me wear it."

That was not the last time I saw Dashan. He was still wearing the crewcut as in the past, but the unsightly stubble on his chin gave him a somewhat dejected look. In his deposition made before Onetwo's court appearance, he claimed that the watch was his gift to Onetwo and had nothing to do with the business relationship between their fathers. The lawyer of Dashan's father also questioned Onetwo about it during cross-examination. Onetwo's facial expression was the most painful I had ever seen—an expression that was even more grief-stricken than the night she couldn't get the tinfoil stuck to the urn. It could be seen in between her eyebrows, exposing the slight dip on her forehead.

No, we fell in love only in May. You can check the date. The purchasing date of the watch was the twelfth of April.

Dashan uttered a roaring protest from the audience seat.

In the end, because Dashen was the blood relative, his testimony was rejected by court. His father was sentenced to time in jail.

After we came back, on this sofa I asked Onetwo how she could be so sure that the father of Dashan was the whistleblower. She took out a black notebook and on the last page was written: "Bai Liansheng said that if I withhold approval of his project he would report me to the authorities for implicitly asking for bribes."

The notebook turned out to be Father Four's diary.

She then walked towards the terrace to water the houseleek. I knew she was crying.

The next day Onetwo went to the flower market and bought a houseleek plant in a similarly shaped pot.

Dashan was later taken in by his aunt who lived in the England. He came to see Onetwo before he left, but Onetwo only asked me to give the newly bought houseleek to Dashan and refused to come down from her hiding place on the terrace. I saw very clearly the mole on Dashan's right cheek. There were tears on it. With that potted plant he went into a Toyota Crown 3.0.

For the umpteenth time the CD was playing *This Love*.

You walked towards the water dispenser to get me a cup of water. Are you thirsty?

I nodded and had some cold water.

I said: This is how the story of Onetwo and Dashan ended, are you disappointed? You shook your head no, sometimes regret may give you the reason to miss something. I said no, you shouldn't say that, maybe this is something entirely avoidable and yet I just let it happen right before my eyes. You sat down, held me close to you, and started kissing softly the dent on my forehead. Please don't blame yourself. This is something out of your control.

I drank some more cold water. I needed to finish reading the last letter for you.

I showed you the letter, with the red bloodstain on it. You remarked that it looked horrible. What happened? I smiled at you, raising the corners of my mouth. Don't say a word. Let me read it to you.

It was, in fact, a suicide note by Onetwo. She was, in her own words, "alone in this world."

"This will be my last letter to you. If I remembered it correctly, my previous letter to you was written in the waiting room at the detention center. Now, there is no one to wait anymore. You surely know that I still love Dashan. He is my man. I used these words when I introduced him to you. But his father is now in jail because of me, and I do hate his father. It was he who made me lose the only close relative I had. By the same logic, Dashan must hate me too. Between the two men I loved, one is dead and the other will always bear a grudge against me.

"... When I said in court that the twelfth of April was not the day of our anniversary, I heard Dashan's protest roar. I was named 'April the twelfth' because it was the wedding anniversary of my parents. I was hoping that by choosing that date to cement my love to Dashan it could assure me that our love for each other would also be as abiding as that between my father and mother. Yet, I know, I destroyed our love willingly and with my own hands.

"... When you read this letter, I should be cold and lying in an icebox somewhere already. The ones who leave first are always the lucky ones. My mother therefore must be the luckiest person. When she passed away there were so many people lighting the points of lights for her. The grieving ones are always the friends, relatives and the husbands or wives from whom the loved ones were taken from. Please forgive me for making you a grieving person. I am now so poor that I don't have even a penny to my name. If not, I will certainly leave everything to you, the only loving friend I have, and please don't bear grudges against me. I am leaving my father's diary to you. Please promise me, and you must promise me, because all those who should be punished have received their due punishment, that after reading it you won't hate my father or me, promise? You have my best wishes and my sincere apology.

"P.S. Please take good care of that pot of house-leek. Dashan told me that it would flower the next spring.

"Sincerely, Onetwo"

Onetwo ended her own life without hesitation.

I took off my slippers and lied down in your

arms. The wind outside seemed to have subsided a little, but the faint swishing sound of leaves blowing in the wind could still be heard. "The story is coming to an end," I said.

Your fingers were caressing my forehead as I asked if you could imagine the looks of Onetwo. Too bad I don't have a picture of her here. You nodded. I have a complete picture of her now. You asked me what was said in the diary in that black notebook and why Onetwo said those things.

I closed my eyes. I am a little sleepy. Dawn is almost here. Rammasun seemed to have lost most of its strength. I could smell an odor of wet tobacco emanating from your body. Can I tell you the story in that black notebook the next time? A week from now, you may come to see me at about the same time you came last night, but don't disturb me before then. Let me have seven days by myself, and I will tell you the story after seven days, but as for now, let me get some sleep.

You showed up again a week later.

I gave you the key to the place a week earlier. You opened the door, on the coffee table before the sofa were two notebooks in black, a letter and the houseleek plant. You opened one up and started reading it slowly. Your eyes dimmed and dimmed further. What a story!

After Mother Four died, Father Four swore that he would make money, so as to ensure that Onetwo would not suffer even a bit. His subservience to his superiors, his extraordinary wits and luck soon got him the bureau chief position. He then got his most trusted friend, my father, to be his secretary. My father signed off on every bribe he took and all the embezzled money he pocketed. Father Four assured my father that all the money would be restored and returned eventually. Three years ago, the audit of the bureau account took place ahead of schedule without warning and my father got so scared that he slit open the gas line. Father Four borrowed the amount of the missing money from the father of Dashan one day before the deadline, but my father died already. In his diary, Father Four was full of self-reproach and regret.

You finally understood why Onetwo wrote those words in her suicide note.

You didn't have time to reconcile the content of the diary with the story I told you the night Rammasun hit before you rushed to open the letter I left you, because you couldn't find me anywhere. I had promised to tell the whole story to you but you could find no trace of me after you came.

The letter read like this:

"Did you read the two diaries first before you open this letter?

"This week I have so many things to attend to that I didn't touch base with you. You also kept your promise of not disturbing me. Two years ago when Onetwo left the suicide note and ended her life I felt that it was time for me to go too. But I always hoped that someone would know this story. You were the only one who sat through it. Maybe you can attribute this to fate, since all the others left in a hurry, I have to live until now, with my guilty conscience as a punishment. Onetwo was right about those who leave early are always the lucky ones. You could guess now that at this moment I have also ended my life the same way.

"My dear (please allow me to call you that), I have some inheritance, which I will leave all to you. I would hope that you would do one thing for me. Please give this potted houseleek to Dashan. He left the address and telephone of his aunt with me two years ago. Please tell him that this is actually the one he bought for Onetwo. Onetwo was also planning to be his bride. Only by doing this can you get my will from my lawyer. This is not a transaction, so please don't feel embarrassed. I think I love you too, but I cannot continue my life, since someone has already listened to the story to the very end.

"You have already read the diary of my father; you should understand it all, the doubt that once flashed across your eyebrows and in your eyes should have been answered by now, but the document with the opening phrase 'I want justice' had already been deleted by me. Please also relay these details to Dashan as well, because I didn't have the courage to tell him many years ago, and I thereby killed their love and the life of Onetwo by mistake. Please make some amends on my behalf.

"I will love you."

I used to be someone who was real to the touch, but now, the blood in my body should also have soaked the cement at the entrance of the old complex. This was the way Onetwo climbed to the top floor of the complex and jumped. She had her suicide note in her pocket, with her blood flowed quietly on the cement floor. Blood is the best dye; it takes many years for it to totally fade away. Now, it will be mixed with mine.

I seemed to see you tearing up. It began to drizzle outside; another typhoon was coming towards us and would land soon, according to the forecast. You were silently waiting for the police to inform you that your girlfriend is dead and they found your cell phone number in her pocket. The houseleek sits silently on the coffee table. You don't have time to think how to send it to England. Maybe you should tell Dashan that Onetwo had ended her life decisively two years ago and I also ended mine the same way on the seventh morning after the night of Rammasun, leaving you at a loss at my place.

Whatever happens, I know that you surely will retell this story to Dashan.

Together with this houseleek plant.

Consequences

From the rising of A, B arises.
    From the cessation of A, B ceases.

Twelve Nidanas, three worlds, two planes of causes and consequences
    The first plane: past causes that led to present consequences
    The second plane: present causes that will lead to future consequences

I was Daughter Three.

I could no longer recall when I first opened my eyes and saw the tightly closed eyes on the ruddy face of my maternal grandma. In a low murmur she was reciting something I didn't quite understand. I struggled to move my two hands as the Buddhist chime roped around my wrist jingled incessantly. My first memory was being exposed to bright sunshine in a tight bundle. It was a handmade dark brown cotton-padded coverlet, wrapped up tight by Grandma into a candlestick-shaped bundle that had restricted my growth. With every movement of my hands that were wrapped tightly inside, the chime would touch the lining of the coverlet here or there and jingle.

Grandma had an old rattan lounge chair that occupied a place right in front of the house. On a sunny day she would always be in great spirits. She would pick her baby girl up from bed, and lie down in the lounge chair contently. She would then open up a booklet with pages yellowed like withered leaves, with one hand holding the booklet, another patting lightly the stick bundle with me in it on her lap, and read the text in a low voice. I would stare at the scene, the strange-looking characters appeared vertically on the pages that looked like withered leaves were the first group of Chinese characters I recognized: *The Mahaparinirvana Sutra*. These characters at the time, like all other Chinese characters, were not at all mysterious. They were as common as the others, except that they were rather difficult to write.

A river meandered through the front of the house shared by me and Grandma, who later corrected me that the water should be referred to as a stream and not a river. Every morning, Grandma, like our neighbors, needed to take the red chamber pot as well as the brush made of twigs, walked unsteadily down the stone steps by the stream, opened the pot by the four pinch holes on the lid and swished it clean with stream water. As a result, the stream in front of our house really smelled, infested by swarms of mosquitos, flies, and other pests in the summer time. Ever since my brain was mature enough to detect odor I became used to the smell and like all kids who grew up by the Liyuan Stream, we had developed the strongest immunity with our sense of smell. The second group of Chinese characters I learned was those painted red by Grandma on the stonewall that stood at our entrance: Number xx, Liyuan Stream.

Grandma was considered the most learned person among the stream residents. We also had an unusually large collection of books in our household where I had my first encounter with the strange looking Sanskrit. But I was more interested in picture story books than texts, not unlike any other kids my age. Grandma on the other hand, were just like other women who lived by the stream, spoke the local dialect with accents and with hips twisted right and left with their every step, struggled with the red chamber pot daily.

I began to grow out of the bundle, started wearing split pants, while trying to get the hard stools out when Grandma was reciting the sutra on that old lounge chair. I stretched out my legs and ran hard along the stream. Grandma would run after me, calling me by my nickname "baby girl." When she caught me she would pick me up and use her dry finger to pinch my behind. There were many wild mulberry trees by Liyuan Stream, one after another. At first, I could only pass two wild mulberry trees in front of our house before being caught. Later on, I could go past three trees, and then four. Every time when Grandma picked me up skillfully by my waist and walked back I would let the Buddhist chime on my wrist chime in sync with her pace and watched the mulberry trees past us one by one.

Erma lived across the thirteenth mulberry tree. Of course my count started with the mulberry tree in front of our house as the first one.

By the time I knew Erma we were both beyond the age of wearing split pants. Erma was his father's first son. He had a younger brother by his stepmother, but the brother fell into Liyuan Stream at the age of two, an incident Grandma described as committing a sin, and he became the only son of the family. Since his stepmother never had another child, she was referred to as the mother of Erma by the people of Liyuan, as if she was Erma's birth mother. Later, a low wall with red brick and cement was erected along the stream, and with different colors of pebbles we found on the ground, Erma and I would crouch there to write or draw on the wall as hard as we could. I wrote out the name of

The Mahaparinirvana Sutra, because I was glad that Erma, who was two years my senior, could figure out only one character out of five. I opened my mouth and proudly told him how to read the other characters and he also tried to learn in earnest. But as soon as he found out that I was merely copying those characters from Grandma's booklet, with a swagger he lifted up an entire piece of red brick, threw it to the ground with all his might, picked a suitable piece of brick shard and wrote: certificate of purchase. Then with an iron pointer that seemed to come from nowhere he said: Daughter Three, read after me!

One day when he took apart a house umbrella he was taught a lesson by his mother using the umbrella stem-turned iron pointer, and it was with his battered body that he went to the entrance exam of the elementary school at the end of Liyuan Stream. I was underaged at the time but Grandma pleaded with the principal to make an exception and let me take the exam, and take me in only if I made it on to the top ten. Releasing Grandma's hand I took the hand of Erma and walked into the place of exam. We actually didn't know that this was an exam at the time. We were seated next to each other, whenever I got stumbled Erma would raise his hand and ask a question of the teacher, and when the teacher turned around and walked back Erma would put his exam paper in front of me. He turned out to be the student who asked the most questions in the classroom.

After the result came out Grandma was exhilarated and passed out lucky sweets to others: My baby girl is so smart! She made the first in the exam!

For whatever reason, Erma was not among the top ten posted by the school. I learned later that his father had managed to get him into the Center Elementary School in town, a much better equipped school than the one at the end of the stream that was actually located in a temple. But when I walked past his house I heard his mother scolding him, "You little rascal, don't you know what's good for you?" as the swollen-eyed Erma crouched in a corner next to the chamber pot stammering and sobbing, "I won't go! I won't!"

The name of the town where I lived was Zhenru ("suchness" or "true nature of reality" in English) Township.

By the time I understood the origin of the name, a truncated version of *The Origination of Suchness*, I had already left that place. It was an unremarkable evening when I left the town with *The Essay in Praise of Buddha* and *The Mahaparinirvana Sutra* given to me by Grandma and after seeing the dark brown burn scars on Erma's scalp when he stooped to bow. The orange-gold sun was shining on the memorial arch at the town entrance. Although the characters on the arch were now retouched with gold powder, they remained as fuzzy as ever to me.

The Essay in Praise of Buddha says that, "The Buddha, who has mastered the true nature of reality and has wonderful power has not been successful at all places; who has reached the state of nirvana, but is unable to deliver all living creatures from their suffering."

The elementary school at the end of Liyuan Stream in its previous life was a long-deserted ancient temple of the Ming Dynasty which was later converted to a private school during the reign of Daoguang of the Qing Dynasty. With a new red canvas satchel I went through the back door of the ancient temple numerous times.

The front door of the temple was locked tight and its main hall was also off limits for us. In fact we only borrowed a small side room of the temple as our music classroom, and there stood a very old black Yamaha piano. Most of our study was done at another three story brick building constructed by the school.

My classroom was on the third floor, the pointed roof with cross beams and tightly laid tiles never leaked in rainy days. During class recess I would play rubber band jump rope with other girls like crazy in the hallway until we were covered with sweat. When the school day was over Grandma and other parents would wait for us at the school entrance, poking their heads to take a good look whenever a kid came out. Grandma just loved a delayed school release, since that would give her the time to bet with other waiting parents that her "baby girl" would be the first one to come out. When she saw me running out with the red canvas satchel and the dangling lunch box wrapped in towel brimming with energy, she would tell me in a face red with pride, "My precious baby girl, Grandma knew that you would be the first one out."

I was always the best student in my class.

Anyone in that age group—me or Erma or other kids—had a natural curiosity towards what was hidden from our cognizance, as if there was a mysterious force driving us to explore and pursue the always tightly-closed door of the ancient temple for example.

The temple door was made of a brownish-gray poplar, it showed no signs of ever being painted before, and it was locked tight from inside. Erma and

I had tried many times to climb over and look around, but every time we would be interrupted halfway by a strange sound coming from inside, and Erma would immediately jump down, take my hand and run, screaming at the same time: "Buddha is getting mad, Buddha is getting mad." I would scream after him and run even harder than he did.

When I asked Erma if he had seen the temple inside, he would tell me in all seriousness that it was eerily dark inside, covered by dried leaves and dust, just like the ghostly temple appeared in the martial art video shown on the closed circuit TV in town.

The aging ginkgo tree that stood in front of the poplar door was half hollowed out by termites, exposing its bloody-red innards. Sticky saps clung to its barks. On holidays, Erma and I often went to pick its fan-shaped leaves underneath, our plastic Mary Jane sandals also trampled and screeched on the yellow ones on the ground. In a serious tone Erma asked me:

Daughter Three, what is that red stuff?

Blood, it bleeds from being bitten by so many ants.

Occasionally, an old monk and later a young monk, and later still only the same old monk would take a broom and push the temple door open from inside with a jarring sound, with a shiny head he would sweep clean the fallen leaves while paying no attention at all to Erma and me. We began to realize later that he was the source of the strange sound we heard from inside and it was that realization that had led our curiosity to grow out of control.

My only playmate before going to school was Erma. He had a mother and a father, and I had Grandma. In spite of the different ways we addressed them, their differences in number and age, it was all the same to me. I never entertained the thought that I should also have a mother and a father. But it gradually dawned on me after going to school that people around me all had mothers and fathers, who also had their own mothers and fathers, who were addressed as "grandma" or something else. I then realized that I was actually different from the others because I didn't have my own mother and father. All I had was the mother of my mother, Grandma. I started asking the question: Grandma, where is my mother?

Grandma never answered the questions I asked. She would instead contently leaf through the lifeless pages of *The Mahaparinirvana Sutra*, closed her eyes and with concentration recited the verses in a low voice. Feeling dejected, I would run past thirteen wild mulberry trees and yelled under the tree: Erma—!

Erma's mother was glad to see me looking for

him. She always referred to me as "happy" in front of the neighbors. She would take out the small table and put it in front of the low wall, and Erma would drag out a bamboo stool from home, holding chess game, war game or flight game in his arms and calling out my name, "Daughter Three. Daughter Three." We would then begin to play, totally unaware of the stagnant putrid smell emanating from Liyuan Stream. Later when his mother got distracted we would sneak out to the more-dead-than-alive ginkgo tree by the door of the ancient temple.

That day, the glimmer of sunshine was in retreat. The smell of salt and alkaline that always mixed in with the early autumn air had somehow stimulated the already damaged sense of smell of Erma and me. Erma with his hand on the poplar door ventured a suggestion: Daughter Three, let us play the game of time with the old wolf. So I took a few steps backward and asked him the time, ready to pretend to be a wooden figure as soon as he turned his head. This was the childhood game that impressed me the most, and it was probably the game that caused Erma to push open the poplar door.

It had always been my belief that although we didn't know anything at the time, the curiosity about anything mysterious or even the urge to verify the mystery was never far from our mind, and being kids in preteens we hadn't even learned to suppress the urge. And that was why we, behind the backs of the grown-ups, managed to move our games time and again to the doorstep of this forever closed run-down ancient temple at the end of Liyuan Stream.

When my question was about to be answered by Erma with the trigger phrase "it is dark," perhaps he was too excited by the catching me part that follows, he unexpectedly pushed the huge poplar door open. I froze on the spot and the possibility that he would suddenly turn into an old wolf to catch me seemed to have escaped me completely. Erma with his back towards me also stood there facing the main hall of the ancient temple, looking dazed, completely forgetting that as the one who asked the time I was waiting for his sudden attack after his "it is dark" response. In fact, we both were stunned by this surprise "attack."

We began to duck into the temple and tiptoed ahead, one after another. It was entirely correct to use the word "duck," because we were good imitators and the way the men dressed in black walking under the cover of darkness in the martial art movies was forever etched in our memory.

The yard inside was kept surprisingly clean, whether Erma actually saw anything inside the few

times he tried to climb over the poplar door remained
a question to which no one knew the answer. In the
middle of the yard stood a tall pomegranate tree with
many fist-sized fruits hanging from the branches.
We started to duck towards the main hall as if by
agreement and were scared out of our wits by the old
monk who occasionally appeared at the entrance to
sweep the ginkgo leaves, "How did you little devils
show up here?"

The already setting sun suddenly managed to
squeeze out a bright light on the forehead of the
old monk and reflect on my retina. Ever since then
everything under the sun became fuzzy to me. I also
smelled the enveloping odor of Indian sandalwood,
the only odor that could stimulate my sense of smell,
it permeated the yard in circling clouds and lingered,
one take of that air and I became drowsy.

Erma and I started to sit down on the stone steps
of the main hall and listened to the old monk reciting
the verses, motionless. That was our experience when
we first entered the ancient temple, as if we were
under a spell. After the last ray of the setting sun
receded completely from the sky, the old monk kindly
escorted us out. He asked: Why did you come in?

Erma responded: The door was open.

I jiggled his pants a little: We are people who

shared the predestined affinity.

The old monk nodded his head and laughed as he walked into the yard, as he was about to close the door he said: From now on, I will respond if you, people who share this affinity, knock on the door.

Erma took my hand and raced back home. I again shrieked after him with all my might. The outside was now enveloped in darkness. As we raced to the doorstep of Erma's house he stopped and asked: Daughter Three, what do you mean by saying that we share the predestined affinity? I shook my head and said: I really don't know, but Grandma has been telling me that I should say that when I first meet a stranger. I think she got that from her books. Erma scratched his head and with a silly smile asked: So should we go there tomorrow?

Yep!

Behind the backs of the adults, we started going to the ancient temple frequently, pausing a long time at the door to consider how hard we should knock. Knocking too hard might get the attention of others and a light knocking might be missed by the old monk and no one would open the door for us.

In the inner hall of the ancient temple was a statue of Buddha about a meter high including the niche, surrounded by the four gods of the west and other gods and Buddhas. The ceiling of the inner hall was exactly the same as the classroom. A fading cinnabar-colored banner hanging down from the cross beam that gave support to the pointed top had the words "Namo Amitabha" written on it. In front of the statue was a meditation cushion with a hole. Erma immediately sat on it and imitated the old monk and uttered nonsense in a low voice. Later, the old monk got two brand-new cushions from the stockroom and threw them on the ground. Don't get too rough on them. They'll have to be used until the next life (*laishi* in pinyin).

We didn't know at the time that he was talking about the next century (also pronounced *laishi*) and not the next life which was a long time to come. So we carefully sat on the soft new cushion while Master Mingjie (the religious name of the Buddhist monk) took out the wooden fish and started reciting the verses. We were free to roam between the main hall and the inner hall.

A smiling Maitreya stood in the main hall. Erma remarked that he was too fat and that he must have eaten a lot of food to be so happy. The colorful paint on the statue was chipped in many places, exposing the blue stone inside and the splotchy outside had contributed to its funny looks. The main hall shared the same ceiling structure of the other hall, pointed in shape and with cross beams, except that there were two cinnabar-colored banners hanging down from the beam:

A huge belly to accommodate all that cannot be accommodated under heaven

Breaking a smile to smile at all those laughable people in the world.

On the four walls surrounding the main hall were Maitreyas in different positions, some sitting, some lying down. Erma started taking his cushion with him and posing like the statues on it: Daughter Three, do I look like him?

Yes!

When Master Mingjie finished his daily lesson he would tell us stories from the sutra that are popular and easy to understand, such as the story about how Siddhartha Gautama came to his awakening and enlightenment under the Bodhi tree, and the twelve Nidanas, three worlds and two planes of causes and consequences that brought all the sufferings into this world, to which we listened with great interest. But we were explicitly forbidden to play in the inner hall. Master Mingjie said that although the old temple was mostly deserted by now there were rules we had to observe, however Buddha Maitreya was much kinder and wouldn't mind the noises created by us kids. Erma plumped down on his cushion again and again and asked: Master, are you saying that the Gautama Buddha was not as nice?

My fault, my fault.

Four years into our association with Master Mingjie, the pomegranate in the yard once again started shedding its petals and unhurriedly bearing fruits. Earlier, Master Mingjie lent us some books in vertical printing form, the same as Grandma's. I said: Since I found the first five Chinese characters I first recognized *The Mahaparinirvana Sutra* on the rattan bookshelf in the stockroom. It was then that I realized that these five characters was the name of the sutra.

Master Mingjie always liked the Buddhist chime stringed together by a red rope I had on my wrist. He said that it was blessed at the Jing'an Temple when he was a novice monk there, and that there were fifty blessed chimes of pure gold altogether and they were blessed at the request of rich families for their children.

Erma held my wrist in his hand. Does it hurt? It has grown into your flesh.

No, it doesn't, Grandma said that it should not be loosened.

Master Mingjie said that he was dispatched

during that ten-year period by the association to be the caretaker of this basically deserted ancient temple. At the time Jing'an Temple was not peaceful either, the stern-faced young red guards often intruded for no reason, dragged out several "bald asses" and forced them to mend their ways. So he gladly accepted the arrangement by the association and moved to this relatively tranquil town with a trunkful of his books. He described the first morning he arrived at the temple of Zhenru:

Basking in the first faint rays of dawn.

I asked: Master Mingjie, did you see the women washing the chamber pots by the stream? You would certainly find my Grandma among them.

Erma raised my hand and shook the chime to make the jingling sound: How foolish you are, Daughter Three, monks are not supposed to go near women.

In fact, at the time I was only ten or eleven, and Erma was no more than thirteen or fourteen, and we managed to make illogical connections between Grandma and the Stream, monks and women, and chamber pots and Zhenru Temple.

I didn't like sutra books, or I would have memorized all the Buddhist writings we had at home. I liked very much the Tang poems Master Mingjie gave

me, and of course they were the poems by Wang Mojie.
Erma on the other hand was very much fascinated by
the vertically printed sutras in complicated characters
squeezed oddly together. So I started looking for the
sutras stashed in a wooden trunk in Grandma's room,
including the old ones in Sanskrit for Erma, but it
was Master Mingjie who read the sutras in Sanskrit.
While Master Mingjie was poring over the withered
pages of the sutras Erma was left dejected on the side
because he couldn't even figure out the meanings of
all the complicated Chinese characters. I only realized
later that Erma was more interested in the vertically-
lined tiny complicated characters and not the sutras
per se, and that Sanskrit obviously touched him even
more than the Chinese characters.

Confusing the primary with the secondary and
putting the cart before the horse happened to me
often later in my life. For instance, I once spent hours
in the afternoon to learn "the four corner input
method" for the sole purpose of knowing the origin
of my last name from the *Exegetical Dictionary of
the Classics*, but after familiarizing myself with the
input method I became frustrated when I couldn't
recall what motivated me to learn it in the first place.
My confusion started after I left Zhenru Township

for college, but as for Erma, I always believed that
he was this confused ever since he was very small.
As demonstrated in his behavior of breaking the
large red brick into small pieces, or taking apart the
household umbrella.

What was my real last name was a question that never
crossed my mind, the idea never even aroused any
curiosity on my part. Those who lived by the Liyuan
Stream addressed my grandma as Grandma Fengyi
and me as Daughter Three. The name I wrote down
on the yellowish exam paper at the elementary school
entrance exam, using the Sanxing brand pencil, was
also "Daughter Three." I only saw the name Wang
Gu appeared when Grandma took me to the Office
of Administration next to the music room to fill
in registration information. After getting home,
Grandma moved the old lounge chair inside the
house and said: Baby girl, just remember that from
now on your name is Wang Gu.

I don't know whether it was because my
handwriting was illegible or I felt no affinity for that
name, new teachers always mistook it for Wang Jie.
Looking back now Wang Jie seemed to be a more
appropriate name for a girl, whereas Wang Gu was but
a combination form of "Daughter Three." But why

was my last name Wang and not something else? Later
I seemed to have found the answer to that question
when I saw Grandma's name on the household
register: Wang Shufeng. I must have taken her last
name. But after solving that mystery I then found out
that the address shown on the register was not Liyuan
Stream and that was how I gradually became aware of
the countless mysteries that surrounded my existence.

> *I'm idle, as osmanthus flowers fall,*
> *This quiet night in spring, the hill is*
> *   empty.*
> *The moon comes out and startles the*
> *   birds on the hill,*
> *They don't stop calling in the spring*
> *   ravine.*

This is the poem I thought I truly understand from
A Collection of Works by Wang Youcheng given to me
by Master Mingjie, as to his other poems I could recite
them but just couldn't grasp the full meaning behind the
words. Only when I left town with Grandma's books did
I realize that years ago I was merely looking at the poems
and not reading them, not to mention understanding
them which would come much, much later.

Erma's fall from a tall tree was interpreted by Master

Mingjie as instant enlightenment.

Another autumn day, the fan-shaped ginkgo leaves with their greenish yellow color gave the entrance of the ancient temple a messy look. With a broom in hand, Master Mingjie again opened the creaky gray poplar door, what was different this time was that Erma and I were no longer watching his glistening head with blank stares and were following him instead. Almost all the families by the Liyuan Stream knew by then that Erma and I were friendly with the old monk. Perhaps it was the almost indisputable safe and mysteriously high position of the monk that our affiliation with him didn't meet any objections from either his parents or Grandma as Erma and I originally thought. On the contrary, Grandma started to become the third person who shared a predestined affinity with this ancient temple.

Master (Erma addressed Master Mingjie simply as "master," which sounded much closer than the way I addressed him), wasn't there a young master who swept the yard with you? Where is he now? By this time Erma already scaled high up the ginkgo tree.

Indeed, ever since that evening we played the "asking the time of the old wolf" game the only monk we had ever seen in the temple was Master Mingjie.

He is gone. Master Mingjie stooped to scrape the

ginkgo leaves stuck in the mud as a result of the rain. He made the mistake of joining other college kids in smashing a minivan on North Zhongshan Road.

It seemed that it wasn't easy to scrape the tree leaves from the mud as one would have thought, as that was an autumn with plenty rainfall. Master Mingjie decided to lift up his kasaya (robe) and, in a squatting position, get the leaves out of the mud by hand one at a time. I also crouched down and joined him in the work. Every lift would leave a clear fan shape on the ground and ants were crawling inside the fan shape. They had apparently lost their way before the rain.

He and I were both dispatched to be the caretakers of this ancient temple. He was also a novice before then. He's got a nice voice for recitation of the verses. It's a pity that he was a bit too emotional. We monks are not supposed to be like that, not like that.

In a twinkling of an eye Erma already reached the top part of the tree, where did he go, Master?

He found the life here too harsh and left the order. He said the smell here was unbearable.

"Pong—" That was when Erma fell to the ground in a big thud, both Master Mingjie and I were stunned by the fall.

Erma fell to the ground on his side. Fortunately, it was a mud ground further softened by abundant rain. But looking at him lying on his side motionless with his back facing us I was nonetheless so scared that I bawled uncontrollably. Master Mingjie let go of the robe held in his hand and quickly walked over.

Erma. Master Mingjie helped him sitting up. I looked up at the spot where he was a while ago and saw a broken branch. Are you ok? Master Mingjie lifted his hand and felt it, nothing seems to be broken.

But Erma remained mum.

I still had a ginkgo leaf in my hand. I used the palm of my hand to wipe out the tears on my cheeks. Grandma told me that I shouldn't cry in autumn or winter, or the stains would again be etched on my face.

Erma suddenly burst out laughing.

Daughter Three, you look really funny now.

Master Mingjie abruptly stood up and walked back to where the broom was. He stooped to pick it up, turned around and said to Erma:

Instant enlightenment.

Sakyamuni Buddha held up a white flower, Mhakasyapa smiled subtly.

But I was not Sakyamuni Buddha and I only had a ginkgo leaf in my hand. And yet that was really the moment of enlightenment for Erma.

Or, I should say that Master Mingjie could see

that Erma would be enlightened one day.

Of course, I only came to realize that much later. I have always accepted that Erma was more agile in his thinking than I was, and he also became a serious and devoted reader of the sutras almost overnight.

The biggest difference between me and Erma was the difference between "gradual" and "instant."

By "gradual" I mean "to move from small to big, learn the small vehicle (hinayana) first and approach the great vehicle (mahayana) later."

By "instant" I mean "to skip the small vehicle and go directly to the highest sutra of the great vehicle." (*The Flower Garland Sutra*)

Grandma discovered that the old monk and I shared a predestined affinity when I was reading the book lent to me by Master Mingjie, *A Collection of Works by Wang Youcheng*. She also found out later that a few sutras were missing from her white trunk.

Grandma started knocking at the poplar door.

She was there to get her books, her most precious belongings back, but in the end not only she didn't get them back, the white trunk went to the stockroom of the ancient temple instead. She started having the smell of Indian sandalwood about her. It stayed in the air enveloping everything.

Sometimes, Erma and I would encounter Grandma there in the temple. Wearing a graying blue dress she sat on a brand new cushion and was meditating and reciting the verses with Master Mingjie in the inner hall, we would move our own cushions to the main hall and read the books lent to us by Master Mingjie.

Soon, rumors started to flow about Grandma and Master Mingjie around the Liyuan Stream.

The town government began to think of ways to make money on this deserted ancient temple. Maybe it got its inspiration from the store front that carved into the wall of a middle school, it decided to use the cleaned-up stockroom of the temple, make an opening on the street side and turn it into a place selling bread. The idea of course would require the approval of Master Mingjie, who was after all Zhenru Temple's caretaker sent by the Buddhist association.

To everyone's surprise, Master Mingjie didn't give the government a hard time and agreed to the idea.

Erma had already left the Liyuan Stream by then. Grandma and I were the only persons there to help Master Mingjie in clearing the stockroom. Originally, the temple had an inner hall, main hall, side hall and a stockroom, with a medium-sized yard attached to it. And now it would be left with only the main hall, inner hall and the yard since the side hall had long been used by the elementary school as a music room, and the stockroom would now become the town's bakery.

Master Mingjie moved into the inner hall, a bed with a bed net was put behind the Sakyamuni Buddha. The rattan bookcase was moved to a corner and Master Mingjie lifted up the net and hung it on a hook. This is destiny, a monk a temple, half a chamber filled with the smell of burning essence.

Grandma wasted no time in putting the old and new robes, cushions, wooden fish and other stuff into the wood trunk in white, squeezed them next to the sutras in Sanskrit. There was also a whole box of Indian sandalwood sent by the Buddhist association every six months. I hovered over the box to sniff the unused sandalwood and the strong smell immediately sent me into sneezes.

Daughter Three, once the paper box is broken the sandalwood will be wasted! Go! Go out and play! Grandma wiped my nose with her handkerchief and pinched my behind with force. I was fifteen, but the Buddhist chime still jingled when I ran.

Shufeng, let her be.

I clearly heard the way Master Mingjie so addressed Grandma, it seems that the change occurred naturally with time. No one knew when he stopped addressing her as "Grandma of Daughter Three," or "Grandma Fengyi" as the rest of the people by the Stream. He addressed her by her first name, and without her last name.

Erma left the town a year ago. His father made a fortune in the stock market and bought a house at the center of the city. He left his games and toys including the flight game in front of my house when he moved, I saw him doing that and then I got them inside without saying a word and closed the door.

Later, I think, he must have gone to the ancient temple to bid his goodbye to Master Mingjie.

And the ginkgo tree.

A day after Erma fell from the gingko tree I asked Grandma: Grandma, what is "instant enlight-enment"?

Just like a bright light, one strike on the head brings about the enlightenment. Grandma was basking in the sunlight, still in that old rattan lounge chair.

I asked Erma to climb the ginkgo tree with me and then jumped down with great expectation. Sitting on the soft muddy ground I was in a stupor. The anticipated bright light and enlightenment didn't occur, instead I felt something warm and wet at my lower abdomen, there were some yellowish green gingko leaves by my heels, the leaf veins and some tireless ants were clearly visible.

Daughter Three, are you ok? Erma slipped down the tree trunk.

He helped me up by my arms. My head was still reeling from the fall, but the feeling of wetness on the lower part of my body was increasing.

Daughter Three, you are bleeding!

The smell of salt and alkaline particular to south China in autumn after rain was still very much with us. I had on a pair of quilted cotton trousers in light brown.

I couldn't see what happened on my back and was turning my head and looking down hard out of curiosity. I felt it with my hand. It was indeed wet to the touch, and my fingers were also stained with a light red fluid.

I squatted down and cried, overtaken by emotion.

I thought I was bitten by ants, just like the ginkgo tree.

Blood! I was bleeding because too many ants bit me.

Daughter Three! This ... this looks like ... like mens—

Erma hesitated and stammered. I broke free his hand and bee lined along the wild mulberry tree.

I could feel the sharp pain in my belly and my face flushing.

Erma didn't come after me.

Ever since then the menstruation pain would come unfailingly every month.

And I never played with Erma again. I didn't know how to face him. I even wondered how he knew all that. That night Grandma said to me:

Baby girl, you are growing up now.

I was growing up. Yes, I later learned that the priority high school Erma went to already had the physical hygiene course.

Erma and I were hoping that after graduating from elementary school we could both be accepted by the same high school, such as the priority Second School by the Poplar Bridge.

Erma was attending the Center Elementary School in the town, whereas my school was housed in a dilapidated ancient temple. Master Mingjie said it was predestination. That year the Second School decided to move the only slot given to our school to the Center School, which means that Center School got eleven slots and we got zero.

Drawing a large circle and coming back to where you started, that was a zero.

In the end, I retained my number one ranking, Erma ranked eleventh.

When Erma's mother was distributing candies around, Grandma was apparently in no mood for celebration. She grumbled: "This is not an occasion to pass candies like a marriage" or something to that effect. Later on, even when Erma called out for "Daughter Three" under the wild mulberry in front of our house she tried to chase him away. I looked at her, stunned. She turned around, glanced at me, and sighed:

Just go then, just go.

I would immediately run after Erma. When I stopped somewhere along the way and looked back she would be again sitting in that old rattan chair and staring at the low walls along the Liyuan Stream lost in her thoughts.

When I saw Master Mingjie took Grandma's hand in front of the Maitreya Buddha I remembered he once said that the Maitreya Buddha was kinder.

The ancient temple stopped its use of the Indian sandalwood incense, but I could still smell it clearly, or think or catch the sniff of it; the circling, enveloping smell that just wouldn't go away.

Some of the customers started complaining

about the incense smell of the bread sold at the bakery. Some self-proclaimed know-it-alls would even say that the smell was the same as that of the high-class toilets in the city center. People thus refused to buy bread with a toilet smell anymore. Officials from the township once again paid a visit to Master Mingjie, but the strange thing is Master Mingjie snuffed the Indian incense in both the inner hall and the main hall before they even uttered a word.

And yet inexplicably, that didn't seem to have helped the business of the bakery.

The neighbors by the Liyuan Stream started telling me to call Master Mingjie "Grandpa." I could easily sense the contempt they had in their expressions. When I told them that all monks took the vow of celibacy (this was what Erma told me), they let out an exaggerated cackle, with their chamber pots in hand and their bodies in a rhythmic movement they walked past me laughing and talking.

I started gaining weight in my sophomore year of junior high school. I seemed to have ballooned out of control. Grandma said that I took after her. She also started her puberty around that age. Does one always gain weight in puberty? I couldn't get the correct answer, but I did gain weight surprisingly fast.

As such, it was more and more difficult for my wrist to continue to be bound by the red rope that chained the Buddhist chime. It hurt and caused a purplish streak of hemorrhage. When I showed it to Grandma, to my surprise, she started crying and said in sobs: I have sinned, I have committed a sin.

From a sheet metal box I had never seen before, Grandma took out a pair of copper scissors and cut the rope buried deep in my flesh, the chime fell immediately into her warm and dry hand. Under the yellowish incandescent light I clearly saw the well-delineated groove on my wrist and its surrounding purplish bruises.

Grandma put the chime in my hand. Baby girl, take good care of this, this had been blessed by the Buddha.

I picked up the chime with my thumb and the index finger and jingled it by my ear. Ding-a-ling. That was the sound I heard when I was small. Now that I became fat, the chime resting limply on fat tissues could no longer make a sound when I ran. I remembered something Master Mingjie once said and turned to ask Grandma:

Grandma, is ours a well-to-do family?

A flash, maybe it was a reflection of tears in the white incandescent light. Anyway, a flash glistened in

Grandma's eyes. She then put the pair of scissors back into the sheet metal box.

It is late. Go to sleep. Don't you have an exam tomorrow?

She stood up and turned off the light. I raised my head and looked at the light bulb, as soon as the light went out. A bluish green light appeared before my eyes which made me dizzy. The room was filled with the smell of the Indian incense emitting from the body of Grandma. I drowsily fell in sleep.

After the entrance exam for senior high school I still couldn't get into a real priority school. Because of geographical limitations, the best students of our small town were allowed only to go to the quasi-priority private high school in the township.

Erma on the other hand successfully got into the priority Second School. Only this time his mom didn't pass candies around. In fact, after Erma moved out of town they have never come back to the Liyuan Stream. Any information about them could only be gleaned from the mothers who went to the city to play Mahjong with his mother.

Their house stayed unoccupied. It was neither rented out nor dismantled. It came into view every time I went past it on my way to school. Those days when I called out his name under the wild mulberry tree were still fresh in my memory.

Although he never went back to the ancient temple, Master Mingjie kept on saying that he would be back.

Master Mingjie, you are not talking about Erma, are you? They have moved and the city center is a long way from here.

Master Mingjie chose to respond with silence.

The bakery was closed and the stockroom became available again, but Master Mingjie didn't move things back in. Maybe he was thinking of saving another move just in case. The Indian incense was back in use. Grandma said that it was the smell she liked the most.

I said: Same with me. Actually, aside from the Indian incense I could no longer tell other smells.

My weight dropped sharply the year I started senior high school.

The scar left by the red rope that held the Buddhist chime had turned into a dark flesh-colored line. The thought that if I wore the chime now it certainly would not hurt anymore was never far from my mind, but the chime was nowhere to be found.

I have lost all memory of it after I picked it up with my thumb and index finger and jingled it by my ear that night.

It simply disappeared.

But I kept losing weight. I don't know if this could also be attributed to genes from Grandma. Grandma never told me if she became plump after puberty, regained her proportion after shedding the extra weight, or became even slimmer than she was before.

Neither did I ask her.

I was used to asking questions after questions and receiving no answers at all from Grandma.

The next time I saw Erma I hadn't recognize him. He was with a group of people holding a five yuan "fragrant flower voucher" (ticket to the temple) in hand and calling Master Mingjie as "Master."

The way he sounded when he called "master" reminded me of the Erma of many years ago.

He didn't finish his study at the priority senior high school. From what I gathered from the bits and pieces of information circulating at the Liyuan Stream, he dropped out because of his propensity for violence.

Earlier, his father embezzled the money from the plant to speculate in the stock market, and when the market was hit by the spilling effect of the Asian financial crisis everything came out in the light.

Everything came out in the light.

That was what Erma told me under the ginkgo tree. Dappled sunshine streamed down through the ginkgo leaves. The tree was no longer within reach. It was circled in with a black iron fence and on it hung a shiny aluminum alloy plate: A thousand-year old tree—ginkgo.

A few leaves fell down and displayed their fan shapes on the tar pavement. High-quality marbles were laid at the entrance of the ancient temple. Erma closed his eyes.

What are you doing? I raised my head and asked.

I was looking at the past. Once you close your eyes you can see what this place was like in the past.

I closed my eyes.

I also wished to look at the past.

When many people were looking to the future, Erma and I were looking for our memories in a place that was so familiar and yet so strange. We were looking for the past by closing our eyes.

In a split second, the whole place quieted down. Strangely, the first scene that appeared before me after I closed my eyes was the blush green light that retained on my retina the night Grandma turned out the incandescent light. I followed the light slowly down the memory lane to look for my past. I could even hear the sound when the ginkgo leaves hit the mud ground: pata, pata ...

Maybe only the sense of smell couldn't go back.

Although our sense of smell had been dulled by the specific geographical environment, whether it was I of two years ago or the Erma of today could tell that the incense smell of the ancient temple was different from the past.

Erma opened his eyes:

Daughter Three, has the Master switched to a different incense?

I stopped my trip to the past, opened my eyes, and nodded.

A year ago I had asked the same question of Grandma:

Grandma, has Master Mingjie switched to a different incense?

That was the expensive agarwood incense.

Grandma passed away in her sleep on the rattan chaise in front of our house on an autumn day during my sophomore year in college.

When I got the news and hurried back to town I was told by the people around me: Your grandma is gone.

Master Mingjie followed by his disciples performed the rite for Grandma. Her picture and the urn
containing her ashes were placed at the center of the
temple's yard. To do so was against the rules, but at
the insistence of Master Mingjie, the abbot there, no
one raised any objections.

I knelt on the ground. I didn't remember if I
howled and cried.

I didn't see Erma. Being the number one disciple,
the indisputable number one disciple, he should be
the first one following Master Mingjie. The burn scars
on his scalp should have been gone, leaving only the
pinkish rings. I saw that some other disciples also
had scars burned on their scalps. They all looked very
focused, followed Master Mingjie walking around
the yard and reciting verses, praying for the release of
Grandma's soul from purgatory in this life and future
lives.

But Erma was missing from their ranks.

The smell of Indian incense filled the air, as
enveloping and long-lasting as it was before.

About the third month since I last saw Erma, or
perhaps a little after that, he returned to the small
town. A simple luggage was all he had with him. He
told me that his father had been sentenced to life in

prison and his mother had died.

He was all alone in this world.

That was the term he used to describe his situation then.

All alone in this world.

That was how he described his future too.

I could see very clearly the green stubble under his chin. Erma was standing very close to me but his face was a blur. Ever since my retina caught the reflected sunlight from Master Mingjie the first time I saw him inside the ancient temple, I became deeply nearsighted. (This is something I talked about before.)

Erma didn't go back to his old home across the thirteenth wild mulberry. He asked me to accompany him to the ancient temple instead. The following words were carved on the red plaque hung at the formal entrance: The Old Zhenru Temple.

Not long after the closing of the bakery, an official of the town government again paid a visit to the ancient temple and talked with Master Mingjie for a long while behind the Maitreya Buddha. As he was leaving, he held the hand of Master Mingjie and said:

The report has already been submitted. From now on you are the abbot.

Master Mingjie replied with a slight smile.

The Maitreya Buddha's smile seemed very kind.

A huge construction project soon followed. The memorial archway of the Ming Dynasty was renovated from head to toe. The street starting from the archway was expanded. Old houses on the sides were razed to the ground and a group of ancient style buildings were erected in its place.

The ancient temple started losing its tranquility as well. The original Maitreya Buddha was considered too dilapidated and was carted away by a blue truck. The Sakyamuni Buddha had also been repainted all over in gold, bright red, and other glistening colors. The renovation work for the ancient temple had started. Master Mingjie no longer had any peace and quiet to recite verses and praise the Buddha. He started frequenting my house. The white book trunk and the rattan bookshelf also made their way to the house.

On my way home from school, the neighbors would advise me:

Hey, Daughter Three, your Grandpa is at your place, stay outside a little longer, or you might interrupt the tryst.

They would then swing their hips and walk away snickering.

I started wondering what was the right time to go home, walking back and forth in front of our house and watching the huge characters painted in red by Grandma on the stone wall, until Master Mingjie came out from inside.

Daughter Three, why are you standing outside the house and not entering?

I didn't respond, just bit my lips. My teeth sank into the flesh and I tasted blood, and then I stepped in.

Grandma closed the gate.

Baby girl, have you been listening to baseless rumors again?

When I saw the sutras and the Sanskrit dictionary on the table I felt that I was as stupid as those gossiping women.

Ever since then Master Mingjie always left our house before my classes were over. The sutras also disappeared from the table. There were absolutely no traces of Master Mingjie ever setting foot in our house at all.

I started the final dash in my last year of junior high school, a dash that served no purpose whatsoever. Everybody knew before then that no children from our town would be able to attend the priority senior high school because of geographical limitations. So the township government used the business opportunity of turning this ancient town into a tourist spot, negotiated a deal with a big shot from Shenzhen to build a private senior high school with equipment matching the priority school and high selection standards for students.

As expected, the required scores for this private school were no less than the priority Second School by the Poplar Bridge.

The private school inherited the examination system of the ancient town and on a sheet of red paper published the names of the ten highest scorers.

Grandma once again passed sweets around and shared the news with our neighbors. My baby girl is so smart. She made the top of the list.

The town was included as a featured tourist spot of the city, and all the buildings were marked as "historical buildings." The archway was freshly painted in a shiny dark brown color and the characters on it were carefully covered in gold dust. The old poplar door of the ancient temple disappeared, and was replaced by a pretentious iron gate in black with two rings on it, two lions, one male and one female stationed on each side.

Master Mingjie, in a brand new gold brocade

vest, stood in the expanded yard along with the town mayor. In a slow but forceful tone the mayor said: In the years since reform and opening up, our town ...

I remembered vividly that at exact the place they stood there used to be a pomegranate tree with many fruits as big as the fist.

Some of the young monks who had their head scars burned at the Jing'an Temple were settled here one by one. Master Mingjie pointed at the oldest one and declared: You are the number two disciple.

It looked as if the townspeople realized from that day on that there was a place for worship in an area where they had lived all their lives. There was no need for the women and old folks to spend hours on the road in order to burn incense at the Jing'an Temple. The ancient temple with its kind new look was receiving all worshippers who "shared a predestined affinity."

Standing at the doorstep of my house I could always see the smoke of incense coming from the ancient temple, circling upward like clouds, but the smell was so light that it aroused suspicion. At first I always asked Grandma:

Is the place of Master Mingjie on fire? The smoke seems thick but there was no smell of sandalwood.

The ancient temple stopped using the cheap

Indian sandalwood incense.

The Buddhist association no longer shipped the incense or things like kasayas and cushions. According to Master Mingjie, all these would be paid for by the town government. An official of the government assured us:

We will certainly safeguard the legitimate rights and interests of our citizens in their freedom of religion and beliefs. It is also the duty of our functional departments to protect ancient sites and properties.

I remembered him. It was he who came to the ancient temple one day and politely said:

Master Mingjie, customers are complaining about the smell of sandalwood in the bread.

The very day Erma returned to the small town he stayed at the ancient temple. The next day, the mothers around the Liyuan Stream started passing the news in whispers.

The son of Ama is going to become a Buddhist monk.

The rite of shaving the head was going to be performed by Master Mingjie in person. This was the first shaving rite after the restoration of the ancient temple.

All rites were mysterious in the eyes of the

townspeople, and the town government was considering a smart move of allowing the presence of a tourist group at the rite as audience for a handsome fee, of course.

So long as I am here, all those who have no business here will not be allowed in today!

This was the very first time I saw the unusual expression on Master Mingjie's face, someone who had been known for his ever-present kindness. From the day the elementary school took away part of the temple, Master Mingjie had always been a compromising, easy-going, and non-confrontational person. But what I saw clearly today was Master Mingjie's red-tinged face and a dejected-looking Erma.

Erma took my hand and walked to the ginkgo tree outside the gate.

Daughter Three, can you give me a kiss? After today I can no longer go near women.

Erma's hair sparkled in the sunshine, the hair that would soon to be nonexistent.

What are you talking about? Nowadays monks can still get married.

I freed my hand from his hold, like the day I fell from the ginkgo tree many, many years ago. I started running the minute I let go of his hand. I began to smell the Indian sandalwood incense lit by Master Mingjie after he snuffed the kyara (agarwood) incense. All my memories about the small town, Grandma, childhood years, the ancient temple, Master Mingjie, the sutras, the ginkgo tree, the poplar door, the pomegranate tree started hitting my retina. My eyes became painful. I closed them and saw the past restarted, redeveloped, regrew, retransformed at light-year speed.

After Grandma's body was cremated, her ashes were sprinkled into the Liyuan Stream as she expressed in her will.

I had no idea why she chose to end her physical existence this way. I had no idea why she didn't choose a brooklet with cleaner water flow, or the magnificently boundless ocean. It was anybody's guess why she chose to have her ashes entering into the Liyuan Stream awash with human wastes and occasional corpses of dead cats.

But soon, the town government decided to fill the Liyuan Stream into reclaimed land because tourists complained about its foul smell.

Everybody disliked the malodorous smell, only those living with it had numbed our senses, or we were not numbed, we were just so used to it.

Nobody told me where Erma had gone. Master Mingjie only said: He is a child with instant enlightenment.

My elementary school no longer existed. Students and teachers were merged into the Center School in town. The music room had been returned to its original owner long ago and now served as a side hall selling souvenirs to tourists. My thoughts drifted to the old Yamaha piano, in front of which I once led the class singing the song *The Cowboy Wang Erxiao*. The administrative building still managed to remain dangerously standing at its original place, although half of the building was already gone, its wall paint had long started peeling and chipping, a pagoda was erected next to it. The mothers were saying that it was built with a huge investment by the town government and that a ten yuan RMB ticket would take you to the slim top of the pagoda.

Everybody was saying that the other half of the administrative building would be razed at any time.

An elementary school established during the period of Daoguang of the Qing Dynasty thus disappeared for good from this small town, from this city, from this earth.

And yet it remained in my memory to the extent that it would appear in all its details when I closed my eyes.

Standing in front of what was left of this broken

elementary school, Grandma, fathers, mothers, school announcements in red, lunch bags, school detentions, all of them once again came back to me in droves, just like what happened on the day of Erma's shaving rite, the world began to quiet down, the noises of recitation and praying coming from the ancient temple were gone, the hawking sounds from the ancient-style new buildings were gone, the words tirelessly repeated by the town mayor, "benefitting both ..." were also gone.

Suddenly, there was a bird singing. It was a canary.

I started panting. I still had so many questions that needed to be clarified; my father, my mother, the address that appeared in the household register, the whereabouts of Erma, and my missing Buddhist chime.

The canary perched on a well-hidden tree branch kept on singing, singing, and singing.

As *The Mahaparinirvana Sutra* says: "For example, in the mountain valleys, the human voice generates an echo. A child hears this and says this is an actual voice, whereas one with intelligence will say that there is nothing real therein.

"For example, in the mountain valleys, the

human voice generates an echo. A stupid person says this is an actual voice, whereas one with intelligence will say that that is not a true sound."

I read this passage only when I was on a train far away from that town, far away from that city.

Only at that moment that I reflected on this passage together with the poem I thought I understood, a reflection that knows no bounds and no limits.

I reflected on the now lost peace at the ancient temple, the tranquil old town, the rotten smell of the Liyuan Stream, the ginkgo tree within reach, the fist-size pomegranates, the elementary school with pointed roof and cross beams, the Indian sandalwood incense, the Maitreya Buddha, Erma, etc. etc., also my father, my mother, my identity. All came back to hit me in waves, crowding each other, and clashing with each other without pity.

The crisp and clear singing of the canary continued ...

(This is the *Consequences* part of the novella *Causes and Consequences*. *Causes* is still in the works.)

Stories by Contemporary Writers from Shanghai

The Little Restaurant
Wang Anyi

A Pair of Jade Frogs
Ye Xin

Forty Roses
Sun Yong

Goodby, Xu Hu!
Zhao Changtian

Vicissitudes of Life
Wang Xiaoying

The Elephant
Chen Cun

Folk Song
Li Xiao

The Messenger's Letter
Sun Ganlu

Ah, Blue Bird
Lu Xing'er

His One and Only
Wang Xiaoyu

When a Baby Is Born
Cheng Naishan

Dissipation
Tang Ying

Paradise on Earth
Zhu Lin

The Most Beautiful
Face in the World
Xue Shu

Beautiful Days
Teng Xiaolan

Between Confidantes
Chen Danyan

She She
Zou Zou

There Is No If
Su De

Calling Back the Spirit
of the Dead
Peng Ruigao

White Michelia
Pan Xiangli

Platinum Passport
Zhu Xiaolin